C. L. DONLEY

Love on a Lark

Contents

Acknowledgement

To the random Italian guy who said "Questa nera,"
to his friends on the street,
when I walked past him fifteen years ago...
Thanks. I wrote a book about it.
If this book inspires more African American women to
get passports, then I have done my job.

C.L. Donley

1

Chapter 1

Adeptly, Dario buttoned up his dress shirt as he looked out across the city from the hotel room window. It was a stone's throw from where he worked. Lately he was there so often he referred to it as "his hotel."

He came often, but he never stayed very long.

He adjusted his tie, hoping by the time he turned around, Angelica was climbing out of bed and into the bathroom.

She was.

It wasn't her first rodeo with Dario. He was a cold man. Ice cold, since his wife died ten years ago.

But then again, so was she. He had nothing to give. She hadn't found that out until she tried to get close to him and found that it was impossible. And she was used to it.

Tonight, he was ending it.

They didn't have a relationship, or at least, they weren't supposed to. He only called her when he needed to. Now they had a standing appointment, every Wednesday.

Today was Thursday, however. He called her at home, and then hung up when she answered.

He didn't even know her last name, because he didn't care. At first. Now that they were comfortable, he wanted to know it, and that unnerved him. He was learning her and she him. A closed-off apparition of him, but still.

"Angelica."

"Que?"

"This will be the last time."

She stopped and stared in his eyes, clearly wanting to say many things, wanting to beg him, feeling the pain and wanting him to offer her refuge.

But she knew he wouldn't, that he couldn't.

Her eyes returned to normal, a coldness that he'd become accustomed to. Then, he watched them turn the slightest bit colder.

"*Va bene*," she said in his language.

The fact that he felt dispirited breaking the news was a dead giveaway.

Angelica was starting to make him feel again, and he was apprehensive to let that go. Where would he possibly find it again?

He admonished himself. *Why do you only want what you shouldn't have?*

She dressed as though she couldn't stay another second, and it tore his insides. He leaned against the window ledge, his arms by his sides, willing himself to stay where he was as she clumsily gathered her things, her garment bag far too heavy for her. She was much too proud to admit she needed help at this point, and he too ashamed to give it.

It took some shuffling but she was eventually out the door. She'll never know how he felt, how he was beginning to feel, and it would forever stay that way.

She's incredibly beautiful, she'll be fine, he assured himself, feeling queasy.

It was true. Angelica was incredibly beautiful. Statuesque, a former Olympian from Barcelona, now a flight attendant. A bit older than him. The age his wife would be now, were she still alive.

He liked older women. They were fun. Vibrant. Passionate. Mostly only wanted one thing.

He liked widows. They understood. Always. Especially if they were still in the throes of grief.

Angelica had not been a widow, however. She was married.

His first foray. At first, he liked it very much. So much so, that he thought he might become hooked. It was terribly wrong and dangerous. Convenient, on some level. Discretion could always be counted upon.

But she'd become attached. And so had he.

Perhaps not in a traditional sense, but he did not want to find himself attached to a married woman. Become a wrecking ball to two families, like his father before him. Angelica was lovely, inspiring even. He was grateful to her. But she wasn't his, and it wasn't right.

If he were to fall in love again, he would have to embrace the possibility full force, not live among the ruins, drinking from the same stagnant pool of the past.

He sighed. He felt himself breathe deep, inhaling optimism as he prepared to go out, again braving the elements of blind hope. It was a feeling still in its infant stages. He had a while before he would need to worry about coming across another woman that captured him like Alessia.

After an adequate amount of time had passed, he exited his hotel and headed in the opposite direction, back to his office.

This had become a routine. His double life crowded in on him. No one knew about his off-and-on intimacy habit.

As far as anyone else knew, he was a long-suffering widower with a teenage son. He didn't care much for his own reputation, but he wanted desperately to spare his son his private heartache. He'd only had his mother six years. He didn't want to deepen the wounds of motherlessness by parading his conquests around and letting them sleep on his wife's side of the bed, the way his father had done to his own mother after they divorced.

When he got to the factory his secretary Lenora was waiting on him.

"We got a call from the hotel in Seoul that said they over-booked, but I was able to get you two rooms at the new luxury hotel right across from the venue."

"Three rooms."

"*Como?*"

"Three. The interpreter will need a place to sleep, no?"

"I'm on it, *capo*," she sighed.

"When will he be arriving, by the way?"

"'She.' The day before you leave for Milan."

"Signora Chambers?" he asked eagerly, "I thought her schedule wouldn't allow?"

"It seems it has opened up."

"Good. She was my first choice."

It was hard enough getting the boss to agree to venture outside of Italy for trade shows and add diversity to the supply chain. If he hadn't found the one available interpreter who could speak Italian, Russian and Korean on such short notice, Dario likely wouldn't have been able to get him on board.

This new hire had worked for the U.N. and had a mastery level fluency of seven languages. Only the best for the company. It just so happened that she was fluent in all the languages of countries that had the burgeoning entrepreneurs he was interested in doing business with. He'd lucked out hiring her and Monday was to be her first day of work.

"Is she attractive?"

"For your sake, I hope not."

"You did not have the interview?"

"*Perche?* You made a fuss, the agency called and said she was available, *va tutto bene*."

"This is what I get for hiring family," he ribbed. His cousin Lenora made a face. His father used to say they were a family business down to the maintenance man.

"Have you got the list of our contacts?"

"*Si.* Park in Korea from SALVA. From there you will see Sergei in New York."

"No issues with sanctions?"

"No. If you would've come up with this plan any earlier, you might've had to learn a thing or two," she replied disapprovingly.

"Where's the fun in that?" he shrugged.

Taking risks. Little to no room for errors. That was the cost of having control of each stage of the production cycle. But it was control that he'd fought for in the last seven years and control that he didn't regret. Products now were cheaper to manufacture, better executed at a higher rate of quality, and it had been his ambition ever since he'd graduated with his merchandising degree so many years ago.

The CEO had notions of retiring and giving Dario more power. It was an inevitability Dario was prepared for. He was only there for appearances anyway at this point, but those appearances were still very important. Dario much preferred to excel in the shadows. But with his stagnant view for the future of the company, Dario had an incentive to let the boss retire.

When Dario got home late that night, his mother and son were asleep on the couch.

Quietly he slipped past them into his own room. He sighed as he plopped on his bed in a heap. He was exhausted. He still planned to wake up early and get some work done while the offices were empty and the warehouse ran.

Only five days until Wednesday.

Wait... there would be no Wednesday reprieve.

He'd ended it with Angelica. And he would be in meetings all next week.

Merda. How could he forget already?

He was starting to go back on his newly devised love adventure. It was too daunting and of no use. He worked non-stop. Grief and professional ambition had sliced through his 30's like a cake. Now he was 42. Still young, in his estimation, but he was confronting a part of himself that still felt angry, still felt robbed. He wanted more children, he admitted to himself as he lay in bed.

Dario only fell in love one way, and that was hard. It happened once and only once in his life. He used to feel bitter about it, as if cheated, when she died. The loss nearly blinded him with grief, not something he was willing to again endure.

But the longer he lived, the harder the grief was to recall. More and more he could only feel fortunate to have had that, and started to wonder if lightning could strike twice.

On the other hand, he had a business to run. A son to take care of. The world needed him. He simply didn't have time to fall for anyone, let alone fall apart if something happened to them. As exhausted as the whole business made him, he couldn't fall asleep.

The next morning he tried to slip past his mother and son to no avail. They were already downstairs and eating breakfast.

"See, Nonna? I told you he came home last night." his son Gino said.

"*Buon giorno, famiglia,*" Dario greeted them.

"Where are you going? Eat!" his mother furrowed her brow, gesturing with her arms.

"I can't. I'm going in early."

"*Polpetto,* you work too much!" his mother exclaimed.

"I know. But if I go in early, I will be done by tonight."

"Papa, can I go out with my friends tonight?" Gino asked.

"Your friends can come to Nonna's."

"I can't bring my friends there, papa. They want to hang out some place cool."

"Your Nonna's is cool."

His son Gino scoffed and looked as though he were being tortured.

"You watch too much American TV, Gino. Besides, you're hurting Nonna's feelings."

"I don't mind if he goes out with his friends. He is young!"

Gino kissed his grandmother on the cheek.

"Make an appearance, and then go," Dario decided.

"Thanks, Papa."

"Mama, go home. We are fine here."

"'Mama, go home,'" his mother mimicked him. "You hurt my feelings, *piccolo*!"

"Leave us be, Mama. Gino loves you too much to tell you himself."

"Nonsense. The two of you would starve!"

"Your husband also eats, *vero*?"

"*Eccome*, he eats too much!   But I worry about you, my bambino."

"I waste my breath, but for the last time. Don't worry about me, Mama, I'm fine."

Dario took a bite of dry toast and headed for the door.

2

Chapter 2

Lark Chambers was positively spent.

She trained two years with the U.N. as an interpreter in Libya and Haiti, and after only nine months in the field, she was done.

She was a failure. She'd let down all the people who'd stretched out their many hands over the years to keep her from dying, the U.N. who'd paid her tuition, only to find that she did not have the stomach for it all.

She was a wreck, deep down. In no state to help anyone else, apparently. She built herself into a monster overachiever, but her shallow-built foundation couldn't hold up the towering facade. She had no family, no roots, and years worth of faking it until she made it had garnered no interested parties.

She thought for sure she'd be strong enough to interpret witness testimony for the victims of war-torn and corrupt countries. She could give back the way that she had received, give the voiceless all a voice. But she could no longer bear to hear the atrocities from their lips hour by hour, let alone be forced to process it, and then repeat it in another language, in a palatable fashion.

Lark had been a child prodigy, but no one noticed, since finding a family to stay with took precedence over everything else. And as a foster kid, Lark hadn't been a huge fan of standing out. It wasn't until high school that anyone bothered to note that she was already a polyglot, with six languages under her belt. And that was only because her home life was so tumultuous that she nearly failed her entire sophomore year— including her second language courses— so she was sent to a counselor.

She had to credit her many foster homes for pointing her in the direction of the Spanish, Korean, and Arabic— but if it hadn't been those, it would've been others. Lark's mind was a tangle of signs and symbols and their many verbal forms. Her tongue had a never-ending thirst to master whatever strange linguistic quirk it heard. She graduated high school with an armful of scholarships to the school of her choice, which was Syracuse. Before she graduated, the U.N. was courting her and she jumped at the chance.

Lark sat at her impossibly long table in the dining room, butted tightly up against the small country kitchen of her Tuscan Airbnb— windows open, a line of laundry hanging a story high, overlooking the old cobble pavement below in the courtyard. A simple white mug with its steamy contents rested between soft sinewy hands the same color as her macchiato.

Her features were dainty and sharp, her movements fluid and purposeful. Her eyes were an arresting copper color. Her lush brown hair was a bit past her shoulders, fine enough that water was no real threat to it— it only needed a little heat to make it shine with smoothness. She kept it pulled back in a demure low bun or a ponytail out of habit, her long bangs hanging down and framing her face. They blew in the wind of the open window.

She smiled and breathed the free air, smiling at the sound of Italian out of the mouths of children on the street below.

Armed with a handful of glowing recommendations and a still otherwise stellar resume, she was back in Europe within a month. The U.N. had given her a tidy severance package, and though she was advised to take the vacation, she preferred to work.

And there was no better therapy in the world than having Italian food and words on your tongue.

She had her pick of the litter at LIST, the linguistics agency through which she moonlighted. She initially courted a job at the embassy in Saudi Arabia. But when the last-minute job in Italy came available, she canceled her plans and had her flight itinerary changed to a standby seat bound for Rome. A connecting flight later she was back in Florence, her favorite city.

Italy was a country that understood Lark Chambers fully, while it may not have always respected her way of doing things.

It was leisurely instead of conscientious, lecherous instead of discreet. It settled matters with passion instead of logic.

But it accepted her, more than her own country and everyone in it. She felt an unbiased kinship, that anyone who loved Italy as much as Italy itself did was inherently Italian. And when she spent any time there, it was inevitable that she always succumbed in one way or another.

The Italian job was interpreting Korean and Italian for Di Rossi Textiles, the 4th largest textile company in Europe. There'd be some traveling, a stipend, and of course, working closely with the CEO.

She tried to console herself with the idea that working for a wealthy Italian company could also be a noble cause. "People need sheets and towels," she told herself. But Di Rossi Textiles was a billion-dollar company, the Di Rossi family one of the wealthiest in the world. They didn't get that way by dressing naked orphans.

Suddenly her phone warbled. It was a text from Channing.

"*Be there by 2-ish, your time,*" it said.

It gave Lark a warm feeling knowing she, Channing, and soon Teresa would be in their old stomping grounds together.

Lark's former college roommate Channing was a translator at Sotheby's, an international woman of intrigue now, currently living in the UK.

Teresa and Channing were coming down for the weekend to help Lark settle in, process the last year of her life, and hopefully get into some mischief as well.

"*Teresa will be here before you,*" read Lark's reply.

"*Keep the drinking to a minimum until I get there!*"

"*No paying for booze tonight,*" Lark wrote.

Tonight she was busting out the gold dress, plus Teresa. Teresa reeked of sex. She always attracted the most interesting guys. She'd been saving the gold dress for a special occasion, a wrap dress she'd purchased in Brazil six months before. After six months, however, there wasn't a special occasion in sight, so she was wearing it tonight. There was always an occasion to turn heads on a Friday night in Italy.

The ogling, whistles, comments, and spontaneous songs that a single young African American woman walking the streets of Italy inspired took some adjusting. Lark hoped she never got used to it. Channing's blonde hair, big boobs and Southern accent coupled with Lark's brown skin practically made them celebrities when they walked the streets of Italy together back in college. Lark had always been a pretty girl, a fact from which she spent her early life drawing attention away, in order to survive. But in Italy, she had been proposed to more times than she could count. By men who looked like they'd gotten bored of heaven and began roaming the streets.

It was during this international sausage party that Lark and Channing met Teresa in Florence six years ago, all of them in Italy doing study abroad trips from their respective schools. The three became fast friends. And tonight, Lark was going to do her best to let loose. Teresa was French and had done an internship with Di Rossi for her degree from Parsons in Paris. She trusted Teresa to give her the lowdown.

"I never met Misseur Luca Di Rossi personally, but he did visit the studio quite often. He's a hot grandpa. Stylish," she confessed over a cocktail in her beautiful accent later that night.

She balanced a long cigarette between her fingers, the smoke mingling in her longer than average brunette curls. She had thick brows and full lips. Her eyes were dark and mysterious, a French cliche.

Each of them was in cocktail dresses, Channing's a pin-striped halter and Teresa's midnight blue velvet and spaghetti straps.

"I think that letter of recommendation gave me the edge I needed to get this job."

"I told you," Teresa grinned.

Lark laughed, shaking her head.

"I wish I was there to see you ask him for one."

"I couldn't do it. I just sent him an email."

"And he sent you a completely professional and unbiased recommendation??" Channing asked skeptically.

"Oh shit, I can't believe I didn't tell you."

"What?"

"He just said, 'write it and I'll sign it.'"

Channing died laughing.

"Wrote myself one hell of a letter," Lark giggled.

The best thing to come out of that shit show in Haiti was the dissolution of the bizarre, pseudo-romantic arrangement between her and her boss. Embarrassing. She cringed as she remembered unloading her baggage to him, almost immediately. And then the moment she realized... he didn't care. He couldn't possibly have cared.

The more she thought about how manipulative he was, the deeper her embarrassment grew. As if she wasn't already relationship phobic.

Oh well. Back to meaningless hookups it was. She'd never had an Italian one. She had a sneaking suspicion those were the best.

"I'm glad I could pass my expertise onto you," Teresa smiled with a confident air.

"And here I thought nothing good would come out of that hot mess."

"Now ladies, keep calm," Channing lilted in her charming southern Georgia accent, "but two of the hottest Italian men on the planet are about to walk past us," she crossed her legs as she spoke. The women were sitting at an outdoor table at one of Florence's small, charming street bistros.

Channing, a loudmouth yet brilliant blonde, was known for two things: mixing strong drinks and exaggerating. But knowing this was Italy, and smelling the intoxicating scent of sandalwood from their table, they figured she probably wasn't too far off.

Lark prepared to feast her senses on the first appetizer of the night, craning her neck ever so slightly to catch a glimpse of them.

While Channing was already in full ogling mode, Teresa took

a drag of her cigarette as she assessed them, as if beautiful men were cheap where she lived.

Lark could barely believe her eyes, and though she wasn't conscious of it, her mouth was probably agape.

"Chow..." Channing drawled more than usual.

"Ladies," the dark-haired one cordially spoke.

Cruelly they kept walking.

They had some better place to be.

There was a first for everything, Lark supposed. She'd never seen an Italian man be standoffish around them, especially a pair of them.

But these men were older. Distinguished. The dark-haired one with the light eyes looked to be the oldest upon first glance. The other was dirty blond, exquisite, not quite old enough to be her father, but close enough to still be her weakness.

"*Questa nera,*" he said to his friend, his low voice a force of nature.

Instantly Lark's heart was in her throat and she felt the blood traveling her body, her nipples. She quickly took a sip of wine, as though it were a chaser.

Helplessly they watched as the two continued to saunter away. The dark haired one took a glance back in their direction, as if he just needed one more memory of Channing's boobs to make it through life. And then they were gone.

"Money," was all Channing said when they were down the street.

Teresa was smiling with her eyes on Lark, her chin resting on the open hand that held her cigarette. The two women locked eyes.

"What?" Lark said.

"I'm not fluent in Italian, but I understood *that.*"

"Understood what?" Channing looked between them.

"You didn't hear the other one talking?"

"No, what'd he say?" Channing grinned mischievously, eyes wide.

"What did he say, Lark?" Teresa teased her, blowing out a puff of smoke.

"Nothing," she dismissed, rolling her glowing hazel eyes.

"He said, 'the black one,'" blabbed Teresa.

Channing looked over at Lark, indignant.

"You *have* to sleep with him for us," she said. Teresa chuckled.

"He's gone," Lark argued, as if that was her only objection to the idea.

"They'll be back," Teresa predicted.

"I hope you're not suggesting that we sit here all night and wait for them to return."

"Don't be silly, they'll be back within the hour," Teresa assured them.

They were, in fact, back within ten minutes. This time, Lark was the first to see them coming from her side of the table, and from quite the distance.

"Trouble's back," Lark divulged.

Channing instantly whirled her head in their direction. Lark and Teresa laughed.

Subtlety wasn't Channing's style. But Lark couldn't fault her. If there were any two men that deserved to know fully the effect they had on women it was these two.

"Real names or fake?" Teresa grinned.

"Definitely fake," Lark answered.

"She's in rare form tonight," Channing giggled as the men drew closer.

"I asked for a sign and I think...this is it," Lark trailed off as

16

she and the handsome stranger locked eyes. He walked up to the bistro.

Channing gave her the nudge.

"You know what to do, girl," she whispered, slowly nodding.

She did. Lark was the only one of them who spoke fluent Italian at the table and typically served as the spy.

Channing already ensured they wouldn't suspect that the girls spoke much, if any, of the language. It was an extra measure of safety that served them well on at least one occasion when a group of guys tried to drug some of her friends senior year.

The two men sat at an empty table across from them, conspicuously. The women nonchalantly continued talking and Lark listened as the most handsome of the two summoned the waiter and bought another round of drinks for their table. Channing didn't know a lick of Italian, but she knew what a man looked like when he was buying you a drink.

The waiter came over and interrupted the girls' conversation with another round, compliments of the adjacent table, just as they'd suspected.

The black one, he'd essentially said. Lark's body tingled all over at the thought, especially down below. She'd just gotten dumped by her boss, and this guy was an Italian mirage. Late 30's, early 40's, impeccably dressed and wearing an expensive watch like a boss. A brooding expression and a jaw like a marble sculpture in the Uffizi. Light brown hair that curled at the edges and what looked to be olive green eyes from what she could tell without gawking, olive to match his gorgeous skin.

He was a work of art, a human ode to Mediterranean masculinity. If he showed any remote interest in sleeping with her, she was a goner. His handsome companion with the black hair and light blue eyes had been noticeably silent once the drinks came.

"Grahtzee!" Channing drawled to the men at the table. They raised their glasses in response.

"*Americana?*"

"*Si*," Channing replied, Lark nodded. They waited for Teresa's reply.

"*Non*," Teresa accommodated them.

"Ah, Francia. *What part?*" the dark-haired stranger asked Teresa in French.

"Paris," Teresa replied in her accent.

"May we join you?" the green-eyed one wasted no time.

Teresa and Channing looked over at Lark who gave a simple shrug with one shoulder.

"Of course," Lark offered matter-of-factly.

"My name's Jane, this is Delphine, and this lovely young thing is my friend Vanessa," Channing began, gesturing toward each of the girls.

"Vanessa," the handsome stranger repeated, eyeing Lark carefully.

"*Si*," Lark confirmed.

"And you?" Teresa piped up.

"*Moi?*" the dark haired one stalled.

"*Oui*," she drily confirmed, briefly raising her eyebrows.

"Bill," the stranger answered, with a long 'e' in place of the short 'i' sound. Lark snickered.

"'Beel'?" Teresa repeated.

"Yes," he replied. The girls exchanged glances. It seemed they were all on the same page.

"What about you handsome?" Channing asked.

The handsome stranger was in the midst of sipping his drink when she asked.

"Bob," he finally answered when he was done, with a long

Italian 'o'. The girls chuckled.

"Bill and Bob," Lark repeated as she looked over at Channing. She gestured in their direction, smiling, as though their aliases were convincing.

"*Dio mio*," the handsome stranger muttered. Lark looked over to see what garnered his reaction and found that he was looking at her.

It was her smile, she realized, after a long moment. She chuckled a bit.

"You are the most beautiful woman in the world, Vanessa," he confirmed as he held her gaze.

Channing and Teresa at the table couldn't help but giggle. Lark smiled. *No game in the world like Italian game*, she thought.

"Coming from the most beautiful *man* in the world, that is high praise indeed," Lark said with a subtle toss of her hair.

"Where are you ladies headed tonight?" 'Bill' asked. Meanwhile 'Bob' still had his gaze on Lark, one that she confidently returned.

"You tell us," Channing replied, smiling.

3

Chapter 3

"So how do the two of you know each other?" Lark asked, striking up a conversation as they walked.

"We are family. Brothers," 'Bill,' the dark-haired one answered.

"We. Are. Fam-i-ly..." Channing absent-mindedly sang. Lark's admirer looked over at Channing and grinned like he recognized the song. Lark melted like an ice cream cone. He was being awfully chaste with his words and it was killing her. She wanted to hear his voice again.

"What do the two of you do?" Lark inquired. The men laughed a bit.

"Why do Americans ask every man this?" the dark haired one asked.

"What, they don't ask that in Italy?" Channing grinned.

"No, it is considered rude. We listen to your accent. We watch your mannerisms. We can tell where a person is from, if they are rich or poor, from this. Which is really what you are after, no?"

"Well in America, everyone works. And the kind of work you

do says a lot about you."

"*Allora*, we *work*, we just don't talk so much about it."

"What on earth do you talk about if you don't talk about what you do?" Channing wondered.

"Life. Love. Food."

"But for real though, what do you guys do," Lark said. The girls all laughed. Her companion was still admiring her as much as he could while they walked.

"We are in finance," he answered.

"The both of you?"

"*Si.*"

"*Beel* and *Bobe*, the finance brothers?"

"*Si,*" he said again. The girls laughed again.

The ladies didn't balk at their vague description. They got the sense that it was more because they were indeed wealthy, and found it genuinely rude to talk about.

When they walked a single block to their destination in the heart of the city, within sight of the Duomo, their suspicions of the two men's affluence were confirmed.

On the outside, it was a somber-looking stone building with scaffolding on the front. Then they were buzzed in and entered the double doors, a foyer, and through the second set of double doors, french doors that led to an elaborate soiree in a gorgeous stone courtyard. There was a beautiful old fountain in the middle, and they were surrounded on every side by tall ancient arches that supported the balconies and terraces of various apartments.

At some point, Lark realized that this elaborate apartment building was, in fact, someone's house, that everyone at the soiree was filthy rich, and could likely tell that they were not.

"Would you like a tour?" the handsome stranger asked Lark.

Lark looked over at her friends who were pretending not to know what he was asking.

"Go, *Alouette*," Teresa absolved her with the French version of her name.

"We are not interested at all in the tour," Channing grinned as she kept her eyes on her friend. Lark was sending her a "don't wait up" look when she felt the handsome stranger grab her hand.

She was caught off guard as she turned to look down at their meeting hands, arousal radiating through her as if he were transferring it through his touch.

She could feel his eyes on her and she didn't dare look up.

Trouble.

She had a bad feeling, even though she'd already conceded that he was probably getting some tonight. Perhaps it was a warning, an omen. It was her first night in Florence, after all. She was jet-lagged, in no emotional state for intimacy that's for sure, and she didn't need any bad mojo hanging over this new job. She needed every shred of confidence she could muster.

But she couldn't stop her feet. She was magnetized by his touch, his scent, his every move and the low hum of his voice, his thick accent like musical notes skimming her eardrum. They walked slowly hand in hand as they made their way up the stairs, the night air on one side through the courtyard's many archways. Lark held the hem of her dress up as they climbed the stairs, keeping her eyes on the exquisite tailoring of his suit jacket framing his broad shoulders and back. Her slightly darker hand still in his. My word.

Don't fall in love, don't fall in love, she chanted in her head. *Stop saying 'love'!*

He took her through a traditional Tuscan living area to a more modern kitchen and finally to a terrace that overlooked the labyrinth of terra cotta roofs of the city.

"Gorgeous," she said.

"*Eccome*," he said, his eyes on her straight hair caressed by the wind. He tucked a piece behind her ear and she was utterly lost. That he seemed to be as smitten with her was the stuff all dreams are made of.

"Is this your house?"

"My family's," he answered.

Dammit.

Lark, you idiot. This guy could be a Di Rossi!

She snapped out of it a bit, trying to remember if she saw any telltale markers: a family crest, coat of arms, anything she could loosely try to decipher.

She was too afraid to ask. The illusion was fragile enough as it is, just knowing that he had a family of any sort. Did that mean he had a wife? Enough questions.

"Is there someplace more... private we could go?"

"Such as?" he raised an eyebrow.

"Such as... someplace where we won't be disturbed? Where we can't disturb anyone else?"

"Why would we disturb anyone else?" he asked.

"I tend to be... loud. When I fuck. I can tell just by being with you that I won't be able to keep my wits about me," she said.

The handsome stranger searched her eyes, a slight furrow in his brow. He kept his eyes on her as he spoke.

"*Mira*, Vanessa. I respect your wish for privacy. But this is not why I brought you here."

"But it's why I came. So what do we do?"

Her eyes were gentle, yet piercing. Not at all confident, yet resolute.

The stranger gave a deep sigh as if wrestling within himself. He leaned in, placing his big hands on her bare shoulders.

Slowly her eyes closed, she took a deep breath. Her limbs were lifeless at her sides when he linked a single long arm around her waist. She gripped him for dear life and let the low tones of his voice caress her ear.

"*Lo senti?*" he began. He continued to caress her, to speak to her in a language she wasn't supposed to understand.

It was the first time she wished that she could go back to age 14, when it was all just gorgeous, melodic syllables. She tried to empty her mind as he spoke. Tried not to hear the verb conjugations that became whole sentences, the gerunds and their direct objects— and good heavens the possessives. She tried not to hear Sicily, tried not to know how well educated he was.

But it was no use. She'd learned them all too well, too precisely, her methods too effective. She was surprised to hear the interpretation was equally as poetic as the unintelligible words might've been.

That he truly meant any of it was probably doubtful. She had a feeling this brand of seduction was preserved exclusively for non-native prey.

Nevertheless, she was unraveling, panting and wincing at the sudden and fierce sensations of need pulsing through her at his words.

"Please..." she moaned. She wanted to know his real name. No way was she calling him "Bob."

But she was afraid. Afraid to burst this gorgeous illusion as fragile as a bubble. One friend or family member coming around the corner was enough to shatter it. If life wanted to hurl her back to Earth, let it do its own dirty work.

"I think... I know a place," he sighed, sounding resigned. Defeated.

"Let's go," she whispered. She took his hand and they walked as if they'd known each other forever, she lagging patiently behind as he faithfully led her down another set of steps, back through the large state of the art kitchen to a small door that looked like it led to a basement.

"Careful," he said. She held onto the narrow edges of the wall until she could feel around in the dark for the banister. When they got to the bottom of the stairs a single lightbulb with a pull chain revealed a dank cellar filled with wines, tilted and stacked neatly in tall, pristine fridges like the fanciest gas station in the world.

She followed him a little further to the end of a hallway where there was a dead end, more shelves of wine and a bar-sized table and stools for tasting. She was surrounded wall to wall and head to toe by ancient looking and curved brick, like catacombs.

There she spotted a family seal: "Bennetto."

Of course.

Inwardly she breathed a sigh of relief.

No doubt he was still in some way acquainted with the Di Rossis. These wealthy families always moved in close-knit circles.

Nevertheless, she felt reasonably safe. If word got around about the loose American whore named Vanessa, she would deny all knowledge.

She leaned against the bar table, the slit down the side of her mustard colored dress revealing a long, shapely leg.

"*Bene?*" he asked, speaking of his choice of venue.

"It seems... only deceptively private."

"*Vero.* But no one will hear your screams."

She had to laugh at that one. He grinned as he watched her.

"Until they open the cellar door, that is."

"And then they will likely proceed with extreme caution."

"Fair enough," she smiled.

"Vanessa," he appealed to her, "I don't like what you're asking me to do, and I think you know that," he began as he sauntered over to her. "But I think you also know... that I'm in no state to refuse you."

"I've never done anything like this in my life," she panted as she watched him trail a long finger down her breastbone, "And I've never met a man that made me feel the way you're making me feel," she confessed, locking eyes with him to convey her seriousness, "but this can't go any further than tonight."

The handsome stranger thought for a moment and then spoke.

"Then I will do my utmost to pleasure you."

"Is that a promise?" she grinned.

"*Si.*"

"Then I will relish it with abandon," she grinned.

The handsome stranger shed his blazer, laying it on a stool. But not before retrieving a condom from his breast pocket.

"I believe, Vanessa, that you and I have a deal."

"I thought you said this isn't why you brought me here?" Lark grinned.

"It isn't."

"You simply like to be prepared?"

"*Si.* Now you know more about me than I know about you."

"Not true. You know that I need to fuck," she smirked, embracing her inner femme fatale.

Lark snatched the condom from his fingertips. He wrapped his arms around her and gave her a once over as if he adored her.

He pulled her close, tight enough for her to feel his erection near her middle. She let out a moan as his lips lightly trailed her collarbone, up her neck. By the time he got to her jawline he was licking, tasting.

Her lips rushed to find his and once they connected it was a like a live wire between them. She moaned again, quickening her pace against his mouth, but he gripped her face between his hands. Gently. Slowing her down again until it seemed time itself had slowed down. His tongue crept between her parted lips. Eagerly they met.

Lark was in a daze, almost in tears at this man's touch. He was so fucking gorgeous and sexy, she was ready to abandon all rationale and decorum just to be intertwined with him for a few glorious minutes.

Maybe she *should* go to therapy, she distantly pondered. Addiction to sex with strangers was not something she wanted to find out she had. But the pain of the past was all so minuscule compared to this moment, the thrill of this handsome stranger's fingertips gliding up her thighs.

He moved behind her so that he could easily slip his fingertips up her dress and beneath her thong underwear, where she was slick and fuzzy, and he let out a string of Italian curses.

Ti piace? She nearly answered him. She caught herself before she could blow her cover, threw her head back and smiled instead as he held her. He began to rub her and she could no longer focus on anything but the overwhelming pleasure coursing through her at his touch, his pace, the carnal knowledge of her body that she was handing over to this man.

She didn't even know his real name but he knew her better than any man did now, even more than her ex-boss who couldn't find her g-spot with a map.

But this stranger was unlocking her, unraveling her as she

quickly came apart in his arms. He held her up as her knees began to buckle and she leaned into him. His back jostled the shelves of wine bottles behind him a bit as he quickened his pace, trying to bring this gorgeous ethereal creature the release she seemed desperately to be seeking. Her cries became sobs, her brow deeply furrowed, her mouth went agape as her climax seemed to go higher and higher with no end in sight.

"Yes! Yes!!" she was crying, shrill, primal, all control completely abandoned. He started to worry maybe the cellar wasn't safe enough as her orgasm shook the walls. She spasmed and quaked against him and he continued to touch her, until she was resisting him and wincing, yet she seemed to want more. Her mouth found his jaw and he couldn't help the pre-cum that was already escaping him in the inside of his trousers.

Not only was this woman incredibly beautiful but she was brimming with sexual energy. He felt like he would rather spend his entire life in bed with her, yet he knew that she was not to be held on to. Like a miracle. And he felt cursed knowing that on the other side of his release there would be satisfaction, and desolation quickly on its heels. He had to prolong the moment.

Suddenly she whirled around to look at him, her light brown eyes ablaze as she adeptly began unbuckling his belt, then his trousers. He was rock hard and her discovery only made the fire in her eyes burn hotter. In a flash, she was down on her knees in front of him.

"Vanessa wait—" he began, but it was no use. Once he looked down he was defenseless. His heart went to lightning speed and he couldn't move, as if frightened, as if being held at gunpoint.

There she was, this beautiful girl with her sensual mouth caressing the head of his penis, the flaming gold dress fanned out all around her and accentuated the toasty brown of her skin and eyes. And holy shit the sensation.

"Vanessa," he sighed, his breath staggered as he watched her devour his length with her mouth again and again with desire and determination.

"*Basta!*" he cried out, grabbing her forcefully by her silken hair.

She smiled devilishly as she looked up at him, panting. His cock pulsated with need, with the shock of cool air and the loss of her mouth.

"If you still want to be fucked you have to stop," he warned her in English, trying to occupy his brain as much as he could.

Lark raised herself up and onto the bar, handing him back the condom clutched in her hand. She crossed her legs and waited patiently for him to finish easing it onto his member, elbows at her sides leaning back onto the bar top counter.

She was quite a few inches higher sitting on top of the bar so that he was nearly eye level with her cleavage. He uncrossed her legs and stood between them.

The plunging neckline allowed him easy access to her breasts and he exposed one of her ruddy brown nipples and then the other, licking and teasing while she arched her back. His hands found her thighs again underneath the slit of her dress and he parted her legs, raising them up slightly before he dove head first into her sex.

Lark hooked a right leg over his shoulder and a hand into his hair as he licked, slowly at first and then with fierce, measured strokes that sent her into moaning raptures.

She just felt so *good* she marveled, reaching for one of her nipples as best she could with her elbows resting on the bar. Her head went back as the need to come again rose and rose.

"Fuck yes," she kept saying. She wanted him to stop so that

she could come while he was inside her. She'd never before had an orgasm that way, but she had a feeling this guy could be the exception. She wanted to have the memory forever, because she'd lived long enough to know she may never again feel this level of chemistry with anyone else.

"I wanna come on your cock, baby," she eagerly confessed. He let out a delicious moan that shot up her spine.

Holy shit, she felt like she was on drugs. He seemed to feel it too because suddenly he had her thighs in a death grip and began flicking at her clitoris furiously.

"No no wait, I wanna come on your cock!" she panted as she watched him bringing her to orgasm for the second time. But then she couldn't watch anymore. Her head and eyes rolled back and the most syrupy orgasm she's ever had washed over her.

She lay there almost comatose, her elbows still somehow holding her up as he continued to lick and suck, moaning and groaning as his desire was reaching fever pitch.

"Now, we fuck," he growled. Gruffly he wrapped his arms around her hips and pulled her tensionless body down from the bar, spinning her around and pulling her dress up around her waist. She was limp to the point that her legs were shaking as she stood bent over in her strappy heels. He started to enter her and she flinched, the discomfort reaching unbearable levels.

"You are not a virgin, *piccolina*??" the handsome Italian wondered, somewhat horrified.

"No, it's just... it's been a while," she hastily summarized. She tried to put the embarrassment out of her mind as she adjusted her posture, finding a position that worked. He slowly eased himself in and out as she held herself still, her legs together and perfectly straight.

"Okay?" he asked her. She nodded. Instantly he pumped

harder, quickening his pace. Her eyes were again rolling shut, her mouth agape, a pained, apologetic expression bloomed across her face as the perfect dick invaded her body again and again. She couldn't make a sound.

"Is this what you wanted, *cara mia?*" he teased her. Silence. When she didn't answer he asked again. A tiny whimper escaped her.

"So good," she whispered as she lunged forth and back each time he pounded her.

Their flesh made loud clapping noises as they lazily met over and over. He gripped the sides of her buttocks, willing himself to keep a consistent pace. He gritted his teeth, laboring in wait for signs of another orgasm.

"I think I'm gonna come," she finally announced, panting like a woman in labor. At that, he quickened his pace. Lark let out an aggressive groan.

"Fuck yes," she moaned excitedly.

Her assertive reaction to the fierce beating he was giving her sex was not helping his control at all. He was certain he was about to wake up and find this was all a wild dream.

"Should we come together?" he gently asked her. Something in his gorgeous velvety tone made her want to purr like a kitten and so she matched his when she replied, "oh yeah, baby, I wanna come all over your dick."

"Fuck, baby you're incredible," he purred back in his heavy Italian accent. Suddenly the two of them began to moan even louder as if on cue. They really were about to come together.

Lark let out a long moan of "oh God" that ended in a scream, drowning out his staccato groans as orgasm plowed through his body long and unrelenting. Drunkenly he teetered forward a bit, panting for air as the remnant of his release continued to wash over him.

Lark couldn't help but smile as he held her close, his exaggerated sighs sending aftershocks to her groin.

She gave a laughing moan as the collective effects of a triple orgasm had their way with her body. She was like a long undisturbed pond, mentally serene and feeling better rejuvenated than any spa treatment. He'd fucked the cares of the world right out of her.

And at just the right time. She didn't even care that she was still hunched over a bar stool, or that her thin straight hair parted down the middle was sticking to the sides of her face and starting to frizz.

He let out another big gust of air, as if having just confessed his deepest secrets. She laughed aloud and he relinquished a small chuckle as he righted himself, disposed of the condom and walked lazily around the bar and retrieved a pack of cigarettes. He gave a gesture of offering once she, in turn, was sitting comfortably at the stool she was just bent over. She made a shooing gesture with her hand.

"That's a nasty habit you know," she smiled with a fist under her chin.

"Not a habit," he corrected her as he reached for a light, the cigarette between his lips.

"But the occasion demands it?"

He took a drag and didn't answer, eyeing her carefully as he gave her a toothless grin.

"So... how did I do?" he asked crudely.

She took a deep breath as if to assess his labor. "Better than I'd hoped so... thank you. 'Bob,'" she pronounced his name with the same long 'o' sound.

"You're most welcome. Vanessa," he said quietly, in a way

32

that had her nipples taut.

Settle down, you, she said to herself. She should be more than satiated after that for another six months. At least.

"We should probably um... get back. Is there a place where I could..." she stammered. The release of all the sexual tension had left nothing but her usual awkward demeanor.

"Follow me," he said, disposing of the cigarette and leading her by the hand out of the cellar and back up the stairs.

4

Chapter 4

"We were about to send a search party," Channing chastised Lark when they finally made it back to the courtyard.

Teresa and Channing were sitting with "Bill" and a gaggle of Italian family members along a massive white table full of food and wine— clearly family since they varied in ages from teen to old age, and they spoke cordially to one another with that deep sense of knowing that Lark sometimes sensed between families. She felt as though a dull knife were stabbing at her insides.

Her friends got up from the table and stood next to her as if willing to leave with Lark, but not ready.

"What'd I miss?" Lark innocently asked. Her friends looked at each other and smiled while "Bill" made his way over to "Bob."

"*Caccola!*" the dark-haired stranger greeted his brother with a kiss on a cheek followed by a light smack.

"*Scuzi,*" he said to the table. He put his arm around "Bob" and led him to away from the girls to a group of older men in the middle of the courtyard. Lark forced a smile and took a deep breath.

"So it turns out 'Beel' here is *married*,' Channing sneered in a hushed tone. "I think his name is Stefano, but everyone is using nicknames here. He's staying mum ever since he introduced us to his wife."

"And they seem to indeed be actual brothers?"

"Yes. I suspect the moment your handsome admirer saw you, he formulated a plan with Stefano to get you alone with him. So they brought us here," Teresa surmised.

"Well, it worked. It worked a lot," Lark whispered as the girls snickered. "Did you find out anything about him?"

"Why, didn't *you* find out anything?" Teresa asked mischievously.

"Nothing that's appropriate to talk about."

"I think his name is Roberto," Channing said.

'Bob,' Lark thought. Technically, he wasn't lying.

"What do you mean 'you think?'"

"I know I'm a dumb blonde, Lark, but even I wouldn't openly admit to not knowing the names of the two strange guys that brought us here."

Lark sighed. "Sorry, ladies. You know I'm the last person to hang you guys out to dry—"

"It was an emergency. We understand," Teresa smiled.

"Honestly, I'm just not myself at all tonight."

"I take it he gave you the extended tour?" Channing gave Lark a provocative eyebrow.

"He did."

"How was it?"

"...Thorough."

Channing dropped her jaw while Teresa merely laughed.

"One more thing off the bucket list, ladies," Lark smirked.

"I can't believe you'd give a man like that a fake name, you

35

ungrateful slut," Channing whispered.

"I'm really glad I gave him a fake name, after what he made do."

Channing gave a squeal of delight.

"Details," she said.

"Marry him, you idiot," Teresa chastised her.

"If by some bizarre chance I run into him again after tonight, I'll consider it."

Suddenly the handsome stranger known as "Bob" re-appeared, his gaze intense, nearly possessive. Her heart went into overdrive.

"Come, meet my family."

Lark seized up.

"Actually, I was just telling the girls that I think I'm gonna turn in for the night."

"So soon?"

"Yes, unfortunately."

"We'll walk you home," Channing said.

"No, you guys stay. I'm not far."

"*Va bene.* Vanessa, I will walk you home," "Bob" replied. "It's far too dangerous to walk alone at night in that dress," he said, only half joking. "Your friends may stay as long as they like."

Lark didn't like the idea of spending any more time alone with this guy. He was already discombobulating her with one look. He was going to persuade her to do things she didn't want, things that would steer her off course and make her late to work on Monday.

He read the apprehension on her face. She looked like she was afraid of him. His heart throbbed. What was she hiding?

"Um...sure," she finally said with a flippant air, as though it struck her as a good idea. But her demeanor was that of disapproval. The night went how she'd wanted, but somehow it still felt as though it had gotten hijacked. Damn. Always a man getting in the way of her emotional healing.

"Ladies, I'll see you... later? Don't stay out too late."

"We won't," Channing said in her sing-song Southern voice.

The handsome stranger escorted her past the courtyard entrance back through the double doors and out into the oblivious night air of the city, the moon high in the sky.

They garnered looks from bustling passers-by in the opposite direction as they walked slowly hand in hand down the ancient sidestreets. The names of the avenues went by, carved in the stone of the buildings as they passed. He started to wonder if she was even taking him to where she lived.

"*Dimmi*, Vanessa. What brings you to Firenze?"

"Nothing, really. I suppose you could say that I'm running."

"Running? From what?"

"The past," she answered cryptically. "The present as well."

"You run in vain if you are trying to outrun the present."

"Perhaps. It seems I can't help myself."

"Why not?"

"Tell me about your family," she deflected.

"What is there to tell? It is large and wealthy. And inescapable."

"It sounds like a dream."

"Does it?" he said, sounding intrigued.

"Everyone wants to be part of a large and wealthy family, don't they?"

"You forgot the inescapable part," he said. She laughed.

"I imagine the close-knit can be a little... confining."

She was not speaking from experience. In fact, she seemed to be speaking from pure assumptions. As if the concept of family

37

was entirely a foreign one.

She must be a goddess, then, he presumed. She sprung up out of some pool or a fountain. The cumulative fantasies of men.

"Where do you stay?"

"Not far."

"Are you some kind of outlaw?"

"No," she smiled.

"You are very secretive."

"Am I?"

"Are you married?"

"No," Lark answered, somewhat despondent.

"May I ask you something personal?"

"It must be very personal if you are asking first," she mused.

"You said you tend to be loud. When you fuck."

"Yes," she grinned.

"How do you know this?"

"It's obvious, isn't it?" she shyly laughed with a shrug of her shoulders.

"*Vero*, but... how would you know the difference?"

Lark's mouth drooped at the corners, a discernible furrow in her brow. "I don't understand. The difference between quiet and loud?"

"Someone must have said to you, 'you are too loud.' Otherwise, how would you know? It would be normal."

"Ah," she smiled, suddenly enlightened. She nodded, as if there was such a worthless human.

"*Allora*, who is this *rottinculo*, this *brutto figlio di puttana bastardo* who shames your glorious cries of passion?"

Lark dissolved into laughter at his dramatic distaste for her ex, words which she secretly understood.

"My... I don't know what to call him. He wasn't really a

boyfriend. We used to work together. He was afraid others would hear and that he would get fired. It only happened once, but I remember how angry he was. You could say he gave me a bit of a complex."

"You must have worked in very close quarters. Military?"

"Shit!" she cried aloud, genuinely rattled. It was a knee-jerk response.

Shut, the fuck, up, she warned herself.

She thought she was being discreet enough, but clearly, she wasn't. She *knew* she should've walked alone.

"I've said too much," she giggled nervously.

"You are far too beautiful for the military."

"Whatever that means, *'Bob,'*" she replied, letting him follow the faulty trail.

"When we get to your house, I want to make love to you again."

She sighed. "I'm afraid one time must be the last time."

"Why?"

"Because you are... far too distracting."

"You are afraid you will stop running?"

"No, not of that. I don't know how. To stop."

He knew he could be the one to make her stop.

He knew nothing else about her, not even her real name, probably. But somehow he knew that.

But did he want that?

"I suppose I am running too."

"From what?"

"*Non se.* You are running from the past, I think I may be running from the future."

"How do you manage that?"

"Not very well," he said, slowly grabbing her wrist and suddenly trapping her against the corner wall of the small cafe, where they first met. He kissed her intently as he cradled her petite face in his hand.

"It's insane how gorgeous you are," she whispered her confession.

"Once more and then I will leave your life for good," he whispered back.

"I warned you. In the cellar," she breathed.

"You said this could not go further than tonight. You did not say how many times."

She grinned. Not entirely sure of her exact wording.

But she trusted him. He was convincing. She sighed.

"You can't stay overnight."

"*Macche.*"

"I don't know when my friends will be back."

"*Certo.*"

"Does that mean you agree?" she said, smoothing out the wrinkles in her facade.

"*Si.* Yes."

They went down a small quiet street just outside the piazza that housed the cafe. They passed a park on their left as they went into a building on the right-hand corner. *Borgo Allegri*, he stored in his mind.

They went in through the building's front entrance, up the narrow winding stairs to her apartment. It was clearly a rental, he thought, trying to glean the information that she wasn't giving.

It was quaint, painfully so. Clay tiles, uneven plaster walls and dark wood beams lining the tall ceilings. The quaint dining room window was still open, with linens hanging on the line. Old world Italian fixtures and an oversized fireplace with modern amenities. An American tourist's dream.

Everything was relatively pristine, her bags were still packed in a corner. She hadn't been in town long. She didn't look to be staying long either. No more than a week, he assessed. Her coffee cup sat abandoned at the dining room table.

She turned and led him backward by the hands and into her room, as if she knew he was doing detective work. Her room was small and narrow with two double beds and a small table between them. It was like fucking in a child's closet.

He enjoyed the challenge.

He sat down on the bed and reclined against the wall. Lark switched on the small table lamp, hiked up her gold dress and straddled him, placing her hands on his shoulders and down his chest. He gazed into the amber of her eyes, subtly glowing by the light of the dim lamp.

"*Occhi mandorle*," he said. It meant "almond eyes."

"What does that mean?" she asked anyway.

"It means that I'll never forget tonight. Or you."

She nearly admitted the same, but instead, she slowly leaned over him to kiss him again and again. She wriggled her dress off at the shoulders and let it hang at her waist, her braless chest exposed. He traced her form with his fingers as though they were his eyes— her nipples, her waist, the small of her back.

This was a bad idea, she thought as she traced the outline around his gorgeous lips with her fingertips.

"I don't know how much time we have," she whispered, reminding him of reality.

"Neither do I," he said, continuing the slow pilgrimage around her form with his hands as their lips again met.

They continued this tug of war for what seemed like an eternity. They shed random pieces of clothing. They changed positions again and again like wrestlers in the small bed, she

41

trying to keep their union from seeping into the dawn, he trying to prolong his pleasure and somehow keep the dawn from coming. She dug her nails into him, trying to hold back for the sake of her sleeping neighbors. Her dull whimpers only excited him more, knowing that if she could, she would be shouting her ecstasy until she went hoarse.

He suddenly became conscious at the sound of Lark's room-mates coming in through the front door and shuffling down the front hallway. He startled fully awake.

Merda. He'd fallen asleep.

From the look of the light through the transom window, it was still night. No later than 3am he guessed.

Instinctively, he attempted to ease out of the tiny bed without waking her. He succeeded and dressed as well as he could in the dark. He heard a muffled commotion in the kitchen, stifled laughter as they tried to keep it down for the sake of their sleeping friend. Then, a closed door, followed by total silence.

Vanessa remained asleep as though a rock. He felt around for the pull chain on the small lamp. Dim yellow light illuminated the dark while Vanessa continued to sleep.

He studied her quiet face, the combination of her dainty features and her full pouty lips that were sure to haunt his dreams forever.

He felt an anchor on his spirit as he resigned within himself to leave her be. It had been a long time since he had tried to woo someone.

If he tried harder, as hard as he could, she could be his.

It stirred him, but the sadness it evoked was profound. Who was he to have this gorgeous thing all to himself? How long before some other man would have the same notion? How could he pretend to have any right?

42

It would take some discipline, but he would pretend that he did not know where to find her.

She knew precisely where to find him, down to the house's cellar. She was a beautiful girl who couldn't stop running. And he, a man too wounded to chase her.

"*Ciao*, Vanessa. Goodbye," he whispered. He ran a finger down her smooth chin, gathered his things and quietly walked out the door.

5

Chapter 5

O n Monday morning, Lark was freshly pressed and walking into Di Rossi headquarters 45 minutes early.

She felt refreshed. Confident. Prepared. Ready to leave her professional blunders behind and knock this assignment out of the park.

She was happy to find that the bustling office headquarters lived up to its high-end expectations. She walked through the revolving doors of the grand building entrance with a single receptionist sitting at a marble desk that nearly spanned the length of the lobby, in the middle of two corridors on each side.

"Good morning. Lark Chambers. I'm the interpreter. Signore Di Rossi is expecting me," she said in Italian.

"You're early, Miss Chambers. Right this way," the reception-ist responded in English. Lark couldn't tell yet if it was courtesy or just showing off.

She followed the receptionist down the quaint Tuscan hallway until they got to a set of tall wooden doors at the end. The doors opened to a spacious office with high ceilings, modern furniture and classic white walls dotted with stucco flourishes.

A beautifully restored fresco bordered the top of the walls and there was a large, unfussy chandelier in the middle of the dark wood coffered ceiling.

They walked through the charming sitting area, through to another set of open doors where there was another large room with no furniture save for a very large, imposing desk. There sat a distinguished older man, with a grey beard, wearing a flawless Italian suit and pouring over several books laid open in front of him containing fabric samples.

"Signore, Signorina Chambers is here," the receptionist announced.

"*Molto bene.* Signorina Chambers, welcome," the elderly Signore Luca Di Rossi greeted Lark.

"Am I too early?" Lark worried as she firmly shook his hand.

"*Sciochezza*, but you are too beautiful," he answered, as he put her hand to his lips and kissed. Lark smiled, feeling a tinge of arousal at the touch of his lips. *Werk, grandpa*, she thought as she sat cross-legged in front of him. Only in Italy.

"*Allora*, you are far too qualified to work for me. But I needed someone who could interpret both Italian and Korean. You came highly recommended."

"No need to explain, Signore Di Rossi. Any excuse I can find to work in Italy, I will always take."

"A woman after my heart! Perhaps we should eat. Before we work."

"Sir, it's only 10am."

"Is it? I am hungry already. I will order for the both of us."

Lark politely attempted to keep her new boss on track.

"You're too generous, Signore. But when do I start?"

"*Va bene*, I thought we would go to the factory today. We have a busy month or so, traveling to Milan, and then to Seoul, and finally, New York, as I'm sure you gathered from your itinerary."

"Surely you won't need me in Milan?"

"No, but you will join us anyway. Many buyers will be there, many other countries will be represented, some of whom we may have the opportunity to gain an audience, with your help."

"'Us', signore?"

"*Si.* Today I want you to get acquainted with more of my team, mainly my son, who will be joining us. He's taken over a good portion of the business in the last five years, and now I want him to have a more... diplomatic role. I want him to be the face of the company, not cooped up in a textile factory 70 hours a week. His face is such a handsome one to represent the Di Rossi name."

For some reason, Lark instantly had a sick feeling of dread and suspicion at the mention of his handsome faced son.

She'd spent the weekend smiling about the beautiful man that'd christened her first night in Florence with lovemaking. In the morning he was gone, like an angel. She'd imagined him as such, watching over her somehow, from a world she could never belong to.

But the sudden rock in her gut made her think that instead, she'd really just royally played herself.

It was much more likely that she had unknowingly fucked her boss's son.

Honestly, which was more like her life? Mythical sex god angels, or messy, ratchet-ass mistakes?

It's him. It was too clean, too perfect. When has that ever happened? You should've known, her inner voice of dread began panicking.

It's not him. It's not him, her inner voice of denial responded.

* * *

Dario Di Rossi had already been on his feet for hours, and it wasn't even noon.

One of the spinning machines in the textile mill had gone down, and though it had been quickly remedied within an hour, Dario had calculated a setback in the schedule of at least two weeks by the time it was back up and running.

He didn't have time for mishaps. The interpreter would be here later today, and his father would be useless in briefing her. But he could barely concentrate because the erotic events of the weekend were still swimming through his brain.

Nothing as that had ever come over him. He'd just broken it off with Angelica the night before, and though he began to open himself back up to the possibility of love, he was still in a mental wrestling match with casual sex.

Or at least, he was until he saw her. Then it went from wrestling match to a KO. He'd never expected to come across another woman so soon and never had he behaved in such a way. Naturally, the moment he decided to venture out and brave the harsh nature of hope, he'd nearly lost his head to a killer.

She was a beauty like no other. Young. Much too young for him. Foreign. His older brother Stefano was a bad influence. He was happily married with a baby on the way, but couldn't stop trying to live vicariously through Dario. So the fact that they'd stumbled on the path of the most beautiful American he'd ever seen on the way to his mother's, made for an inevitable fall off the wagon.

He didn't return to his mother's house that weekend. He hadn't even come in to work on his day off, like he usually did. He was beside himself. He simply felt fatigued, almost flu-like. He spent the next two evenings moping around his villa like a teenager with nothing else to worry about, jacking off and looking up Borgo Allegri via satellite images on the internet. It was as though her youthfulness had infected him as well.

Yes, she was much too young. Younger than his own wife had been when she died, destined never to grow old. The naivete in her eyes was nearly painful to recall. She'd never been loved. Never lost. And she looked terrified. Like a baby goat that'd lost its herd. He had a habit of telling himself he was still young until he saw her. Then he knew he was in denial.

He nearly stayed in bed when Monday came, but instead, he got up and dressed. He cooked and splashed water on his face as he looked in the mirror. Slowly, he felt better.

Women, he mused. It was the hangover that reminded you why you'd stopped drinking. He couldn't wait for the work week to rescue him from his wretched romantic bender.

And Monday had delivered. It was going to be another long, lunchless day.

"*Capo, your father is here. With a woman, the translator,*" Dario's floor supervisor informed him in Italian.

"The Interpreter. Keep them busy, I need to get quality back on track before end of business in Crete. Otherwise, we'll have to delay their shipment."

"What's the difference?" she asked.

"*Como?*"

"I said translator, and you said, 'interpreter.'"

"A translator works with the written word. Interpreters are very picky about the distinction."

"She is very beautiful."

Dario's heart skipped about three beats.

He looked at his floor supervisor carefully. But he didn't say anything.

"I thought you would want to be warned, signore," she

grinned devilishly before returning to the floor.

It couldn't be, he thought.

But his heart wouldn't slow down, and he was suddenly stuck to the floor like cement.

When they turned the corner, he looked up in time to see his father coming his way, past the raw cotton bales and the thread machines, past the fabric printing, approaching Dario's offices.

Behind him was Vanessa, dressed neatly in a crisp white shirt and a charcoal colored pencil skirt, her hair pinned back demurely with a few strands framing her gorgeous face. She had a bit of a dour and serious look on her face and she appeared to be listening intently while his father spoke over his shoulder to her excitedly, fully in Italian.

He was in a dream. He was asleep right now. No way this was real.

His father finally made eye contact and gestured toward him with a smile. Vanessa met his eyes and it churned his guts.

She didn't look surprised.

In fact, all familiarity had been erased from them. Violently. And he knew what to do.

"Signorina Chambers, meet my son Dario Di Rossi. He will be traveling with us while I show him off to our clients and teach him more of my side of the business."

Vanessa extended her hand for him to shake and smiled cordially. He accepted it in disbelief, a shiver going through him at the reunion of their hands.

"*Ciao.*"

"*Piacere*, Signorina Chambers."

"Call me Lark, please," she said.

"*Allodola*?" he asked, the Italian translation of the bird's name.

His father smiled a bit. He knew she was far too beautiful for his son not to take notice. He was already giving her pet names.

"If you wish," Lark gave a little laugh.

"Perhaps... *Alouette*," he answered, remembering her French companion addressing her as such the night of the party. *Che idiota!*

"*Oui, Frances, do you speak it?*" she unflinchingly rattled on in French, cordially smiling as if intrigued by his knowledge of languages. It was her entire wheelhouse, after all. He'd hired her himself.

Moreover, she acted as though she had indeed never even met him, as if they had never tasted each other and that she had less than a mild interest in the notion.

In short, she was beyond professional. She did not want him. She wanted this job. And she was determined to prove that she could not be rattled.

"*Non.* Which is why we hired you," he grinned.

"Of course," she chuckled, finally releasing her smooth hand from his grip.

"*Va bene*, I want to show Miss Chambers the rest of the factory. And afterward, we will take Miss Chambers to dinner."

"Impossible, one of the machines went down this morning, it will be another late night for me to get the shipment out for Greece," he replied.

"Working, working. Like a poor American. You work harder than the last three Di Rossi's combined, Roberto."

There was that name again.

"Roberto?" Lark prompted him.

"My middle name," he informed her. "To avoid confusion. There are several Dario DiRossis among our family."

Her friends had heard right, that night of the party.

"The world has changed, papa. I keep telling you this."

"*Si*. And tomorrow we will change with it. Tonight, I will keep Lark all to myself," Signore De Rossi teased.

"In Italiano, please gentleman. Let me at least pretend to be working," Lark smiled charmingly.

"Tomorrow you work, tonight we eat. Roberto?"

"I will do my best to be there."

"Which means he will cancel. *Va bene*, I know I can't talk you out of it. Let us get out of your hair. Lark, would you like to feel the most luxurious Egyptian cotton you've ever felt against your skin?"

Easy old man, Dario thought.

He didn't know how this was going to work, but he was too busy to worry about it today.

If her demeanor this weekend was any indication, Lark wasn't letting anything get in the way of her career. Not even a rich, gorgeous Italian that told her she was the most beautiful woman in the world before making love to her in the cellar.

For now, she would have to stay, he conceded. Somewhat reluctantly.

But only somewhat.

* * *

"Not only do we supply fabrics for clothing, but for curtains and upholstery, toweling and bedding, accessories and only the finest materials. Cotton, wool, mohair, and the finest synthetics as well."

"*Scusi*, where's your bathroom, Signore?" Lark began.

"*Mi dispiace, signorina.* Down the hall and to the right."

She'd had to pee for over an hour. She thought she'd be able to wait until after they'd left the factory, but after nearly three hours, he'd bought lunch for the entire floor and they were still there, meeting and greeting and chatting.

Shit. She really didn't want to chance running into "Bob"... Dario... Mr. Di Rossi, alone. Now or ever.

You can do this job, was the only inner thought she was allowing herself to repeat at the moment. Even though inwardly her dignity was crumbling, like trying to piece back together a priceless sculpture in a museum that she'd inadvertently toppled. She tried not to think about the thousand pounds of anxiety she inadvertently added to her last minute, supposedly stress-free Italian assignment.

Once she got to the bathroom she couldn't resist giving herself a good long reprimanding look in the mirror.

She closed the door and locked it.

"You dumb cunt," she whispered to herself.

Tears formed in the eyes of her reflection as if she'd successfully hurt her own feelings.

How could she have sabotaged herself so thoroughly? She'd done everything she could to stave off whatever wicked chaos flowed through her genes— on both sides. Tried to choose her destiny the same way the system chose for her all those years. But life, it seemed had other plans. And jokes, apparently. No matter where she ran, the chaos followed. No matter how she changed her surroundings, the chaos drew her. Would she ever be in her own charge?

She did her business and then hurriedly avoided her reflection altogether, lathering her hands as she shook her head in amused disbelief.

Was this to be the strategy? Avoid mirrors for the rest of the trip?

Lark gave herself another look with an exasperated sigh, fighting off mental torment. She gripped the sides of the Italian marble countertop.

Five seconds and then you have to pull it together, she told herself. She crumpled a little bit as she leaned her head on the mirror in front of her.

3...2...1.

She finished washing her hands then retreated out of the bathroom door.

There he was. Standing in the doorway. She jumped.

"Vanessa," he began.

"It's Miss Chambers. Lark," she corrected him.

"Of course. I meant—"

"I think you have me confused with someone else entirely."

"Do I?"

"Yes," she replied. He studied her with his pale green eyes until her pulse was on the rise.

"Have you been crying?"

"No."

"How long have you known?"

"That you were my boss? About as long as you have."

"Really," he asked in disbelief.

"No," she sighed, exasperated, "you're right, the jig is up. I work for the C.I.A. Which is why I was sitting outside the cafe with my friends for an hour, waiting for you to spot me randomly and stop to talk to me. We've had our eye on you for a long time—"

"*Va bene, va bene,*" he said, raising his hands in surrender before she could go any further. He stifled a grin.

"Your family's house?"

"*Como?*"

"You said... you told me that was your family's house."

"*Si*. My mother's."

The family crest. Bennetto.

His mother must have remarried. *Merda*!

"And your 'brother'? 'Bill'?"

"Stefano. He is my stepbrother. I have known him since I was a boy."

Lark sighed a deep sigh and shook her head, trying not to get dragged back to the tempting pit of punishing herself.

"You said you worked in the military," he said.

"I never confirmed that."

"Okay," he conceded. "But obviously, you gave me a fake name. I had no intentions of deceiving you, *cara*. In fact, I—"

"*Allora, I hope you can make it to dinner tonight*," she continued in flawless Italian. "*I'm looking forward to learning more about your industry. The more terminology I can learn, the better I'll be able to do my job. And I can do my job, sir.*"

"I have no doubt. It's why we hired you," he answered back, thinking of all the things he'd said to her that weekend, knowing now that she understood every word.

He had no regrets. In fact, it relieved him. There was now no unsaid thing between them. Perhaps they *could* work together.

"*Molto bene*. Excuse me," she politely said as she made her way around him and back to the factory floor.

He studied the curve of her ass in the pencil skirt as she walked away.

It was a good skirt. Expensive. But her shirt was off the rack.

Was he really going to spend the next three weeks trying not to touch the most beautiful woman in the world? Again? His heart skipped a beat as he thought of seeing her naked once more— fully this time and wrapped in one of his fabrics. He unconsciously relinquished a goofy smirk.

He would definitely be skipping dinner tonight.

6

Chapter 6

Signore Luca Di Rossi took Lark to a busy trattoria near San Lorenzo square for dinner, where space was limited due to its famous chocolate torte.

The owner was a short, pudgy balding man, an old friend of Di Rossi's who wouldn't stop staring at Lark. She smiled as Signor Di Rossi introduced the two of them.

"Vito, this is Signorina Chambers, she will be working with Roberto and I in Korea."

"*Ciao, Bella!*" he exclaimed, kissing her on both cheeks. "Please, I make you anything you want."

They sat at a small outside table where the owner brought them prosciutto and melon. When Lark ordered in perfect Italian, he suddenly grabbed her by her face and pulled her close to him, his rotund chest eye level to her from where she sat.

Aside from a cordial smile from the senior Mr. Di Rossi, no one batted an eye. Lark righted herself when he finally let her go, smoothing her hair as she politely smiled.

With Dario not present, it wasn't long before the dinner conversation became gossip.

"*Allora*, enough business talk, it is boring. What did you think of my son?"

She laughed, feeling a bit put on the spot. At least she could pretend with Luca Di Rossi that she still had her dignity. She could use the practice.

"I prefer to keep things professional, signore," she replied.

"*Certamente*, this is what I meant, what else?" he innocently replied. She smiled.

"He's... very impressive, Signore Di Rossi."

"I have a feeling he also finds you equally... impressive, signorina," he said with a raise eyebrow.

Lark merely giggled politely in response before taking another sip of wine. He had no idea that Dario Di Rossi had already had a chance to form an opinion of her. And she suspected it wasn't so flattering.

"Okay, *va bene*, I confess," he continued, "I think there may be a spark between you two. Did you not feel it?"

She squirmed under the frankness of the conversation. There were some things about Italians she wasn't completely on board with.

"Signore, please, I am far too reserved for this conversation."

"I think I have my answer," he teased her. "Indulge me, signorina. We will never have another chance to speak alone on this trip. I am curious to know an outsider's impression of him."

"He appears to keep his cards very close to his chest," she volunteered, thinking more of the man she met that weekend, "do you know the saying?"

"*Si*, and you are right. You must excuse him, signorina, he seems a little more grumpy than usual. He is not accustomed to beautiful women who are not so easily affected by him, I think."

Lark surrendered another laugh. "Oh, not to worry, he was very cordial, more than pleasant. I just hope we will be able to work together in a professional capacity."

"*Certo*, why would you not?"

Lark stiffened. She felt as though she'd practically confessed to their weekend fling.

"Well... I just meant... if he is so proud as you say, I hope he can put behind his personal feelings so that we can work closely together."

"Oh no, he is not proud. He is in mourning."

Lark stopped mid-gulp of her table wine.

"Mourning?"

"His wife. It has been many years since she died," he explained, stirring his coffee with a miniature spoon. "Alessia. She was a Bertello, very wealthy. It was a perfect match, they were a perfect couple. Roberto, he loves very hard. *Intensamente*, no? But he refuses to move on. He has a son, so he feels justified to waste his youth and not replace his wife."

Lark found this new insight into him hopelessly intriguing, and a little scary.

A son?

So he did have a family, just not in the way she assumed.

But was Signore Di Rossi telling her that Dario hadn't been with another woman since his wife died? No, that's ridiculous.

Oh no. What if she had inadvertently ended the drought with her seductive antics?

She eyed the table as shame flooded her anew.

She was seriously considering calling LIST and telling them that she couldn't do this job. It was less than 24 hours away from starting, so that would be difficult. But not impossible.

But... she'd already told Dario that she *could* do it, she recalled.

She couldn't up and bail now. The way she'd bailed in Haiti. Largely because of *another* boss she'd crossed the line with.

Jesus, this was a *pattern*, wasn't it?

She was fucked. *She* was a mess. It wasn't Haiti, it was her.

"Are you okay, signora?" Mr. Di Rossi furrowed his brow in concern.

"What? Yes, it's just... I'm sorry, I had no idea. That he was grieving his wife. How did she die?"

"Heart failure. The best doctors in the world were unable to save her."

"How odd. She must've been young."

"She was. It was genetic. A valve. Very rare."

Lark was overcome with sympathy for him. At first sight, she wouldn't have guessed in a million years that he would ever be married, let alone have a son.

She shivered, thinking of how they both seemed to be a million miles away from their true identities that night.

"How old is his son?"

"Seventeen. Gino is almost a man now, and then Roberto will be alone. It is not good for him. Plus, he works too much, so I worry. His mother, she is crazy," he said, making the spiral gesture with his finger near his head. "Roberto depends on her and she does not want to lose him. Me, Bennetto, she has driven us all to an early grave over her children. I wonder sometimes if she would even lay in his bed."

Ooookey doke, the conversation was getting hella personal.

Lark had already deduced that the senior Mr. Di Rossi was one of those gregarious, oversharing types. Her direct opposite and occasional nemesis. She thought the best way to handle him was to steer him in another direction, rather than to try and explain that some people would rather stab themselves with letter openers than discuss intimate matters with strangers.

"What about you," she volunteered, "why have you not remarried?"

"Are you curious how you can win my affections, signorina?" he grinned.

"Commoners like myself prefer meaningless one night stands," she dared an ironic joke. He laughed aloud.

"Do not say such things, they break my heart," he said, holding his chest. "If I were a young man, I would propose to you right here and now. I would make sure you were constantly swollen with a child in your belly. You would be such a glowing mother."

Lark squirmed under his completely wrong impression of her that he'd gathered solely by her appearance alone.

"I'm afraid I'm not very maternal, signore. But I appreciate the compliment."

"I loathed being married. Women are too much trouble," he said, completely changing his position. Lark laughed.

"You contradict yourself, signore."

"Not at all," he said, "I see a woman like you, and I see a one in a million beauty. Not unlike Alessia, *buonanima*," he said, making a Catholic cross gesture. "She also was smart and did not impress so easy," he said, taking a drink of his wine.

"But I certainly don't come from a wealthy family. If it's possible to come from less than money, then that's where I come from," she said, pushing the last of her veal around her plate. "The best I could hope for is to translate for those with money."

"Consider yourself lucky, signorina. The poor can make love and marry for love. They are free. I was much too weak as a young man. I am shackled to the pleasure of others," he divulged.

"I should never have agreed to marry Dario's mother, but what could I do? It was arranged when we were teenagers. Marriage was very strict back then."

The old man sighed, giving her a woebegone look. A bit of Dario's strong features protruded from his countenance. No doubt he was once a handsome man, but he lacked the presence of his son, and certainly all of the mystery.

"Forgive me, if I make you uncomfortable signorina, it is just that you remind me of a period of my life that I took no part in and then threw away. For this reason I tend to live through my son. He has his mother's dominance. He could have the whole world with this, so sometimes I have to want it for him."

She had to admit that on some level she did pity him. The wisdom of old age seemed to torture him endlessly.

"I find your candor a rare amusement, Signore Di Rossi," she offered diplomatically.

"If I had lost a woman like you, as Roberto had, perhaps I would not be strong enough to love again," he thoughtfully offered.

"So you do understand your son."

"Perhaps, but still. I would not be surprised if you become my daughter-in-law."

Fuck's sake, Lark thought. Italian men are off the chain, and not in a good way. Everything was beautiful women and family and birthing babies.

The tidbit about Dario was interesting, she had to admit, but she wondered how his opinion would change if he knew that they'd already shagged in his ex-wife's wine cellar.

"Does it even matter what *I* think?" she teased.

"He is a good man. Tall and handsome and filthy rich. What is not to love? He married properly, and it ended in tragedy. The

Bertellos have their heir. If anyone in the family tried to deny him true love at this stage, they would disgrace themselves. If he tries to woo you, you will be as powerless as Alessia was."

"Your son seems lovely, Mr. Di Rossi," Lark concluded, ready to change subjects, "but nevertheless, you are my boss, which makes him also my boss, and I would never compromise my professionalism," she said. Her tongue was thick with guilt.

"Perhaps, but he will only be your boss for three weeks."

"If I may say signore, I think you're underestimating the power of grief. If he loves as hard as you say, then perhaps he does not want to expose himself to loss like that again."

"You are insightful, signorina," he said, a faint glimmer in his eye, "but I hope, for both your sakes, that you are wrong."

* * *

The next morning they took a train into Milan. Lark wore a gray pantsuit, her hair in a low ponytail. She spent the morning looking out of the train window at the passing countryside. Dario spent the morning looking at the walking contradiction that was Lark.

If he didn't know any better, he would think she wasn't the same woman.

He had to deduce that the woman he saw that weekend was the Miss Hyde to her Dr. Jekyll. It was still sexy, but now that he was her superior, he was invested in her, and opposed to whatever could hinder her performance. Which, unfortunately, was him.

She assured him that she could be professional and so far, he was convinced. She meant business. Never mind that her energy around him had gone the furthest it could get from attraction.

Her headphones made small talk an impossibility. He hoped

that wasn't her strategy for the remainder of their time together. Eventually they would have to talk. She was doing her best to ignore him at the moment, which made him smirk a bit in amusement as he perused the paper, sitting diagonal from her on the train.

"You are far too distracting," she'd told him that night. Only to discover that all her discretion was in vain. Poor girl. His smirk widened.

He looked at his newspaper but the words looked like non-sense, as his mind was now firmly adrift. In two hours, they arrived at the trade show in Milan.

The Di Rossi team was already there with their own booth setup taking up nearly the entire east floor wing. There were more brands represented than Lark could shake a stick at. She'd never seen so many beautiful fabrics and materials, all in raw form, yet to be realized.

She'd visited a number of cities in Italy before, but never this one. Despite being at the top of her wish list at the time. Lark had a handful of job offers overseas before senior year was over, and one of them was in Milan, as a teacher. Before Channing had taken the ex-pat plunge, Lark had already pioneered the idea of moving out of the U.S. to live internationally.

It was a no brainer. She had her eye on Tuscan property when the opening came available at the U.N. She hadn't expected to reach her humanitarian goals so soon. She couldn't pass up the extensive training she'd receive over the next two years. Sure, it was domestic, but once she became an official interpreter, she'd never have to see the U.S. again if she didn't want to. And right now, she didn't want to. She'd never associated a place with more disaster and heartache than America. With the abandonment that always preceded the look of adults talking quietly in another part of the room.

She hadn't expected it, but the instant she left for another country it was as though that feeling couldn't legally follow her. Had her hard work really paid off? Could she really leave her broken past behind? Be an entirely other human?

For a while, it seemed possible. But only for a while.

Lark accompanied Dario as they made their way around the convention center. Dario made introductions and the occasional fabric lesson. Everyone recognized Dario right away as a Di Rossi. They were all in the industry, of course, but Lark couldn't help but be annoyed with Teresa. Why hadn't she recognized him on sight?

"My friend Teresa interned for your company when she was a student at Parsons."

"Really? Perhaps I know her."

"Doubtful. You didn't recognize her Friday night."

Dario smiled. It was her only acknowledgement of their actual first meeting. He gave her a wicked glare that she tried to ignore.

"The American or the Frenchwoman?"

"The French one."

"Daphne."

"We've used those names as our aliases for years."

"Years?"

"We met in college. Studying abroad in Florence."

"I understand now. You get together and have hijinx."

"Indeed, *bravo*," Lark smiled at his use of the word. "We haven't seen each other since I started at the U.N. after graduation. We're a bad influence on each other, but we can't help it. Teresa always gets us in trouble, especially."

"Did Teresa work at the factory or the studio?"

"I'm not sure. I believe I heard her mention the studio."

"This also was several years ago?"

"Four. She mentioned your father, but not you."

"We would not have met. Four years ago I was still trying to get my hands on our own source of wool. My father considered anything beyond the retail process a waste of time. Most of the Di Rossis before me also did."

"Signore Di Rossi tells me you want Di Rossi textiles to venture into fashion design."

"When Di Rossi began, they used to be one and the same. Men's suits and tailoring. My grandfather was the one to diversify it. We are already in clothing manufacturing. Castillo Collection. A few others. But the brands are... dowdy. On purpose. In other parts of the world, where it sells. Away from Italian eyes."

"And this trip. You plan to court the designers yourself?"

"*Si*."

"Isn't it usually the other way around?"

"It is, but we are not exactly a household name to the average consumer."

"That's what you want? To be a household name?"

"Among other things."

"You're very ambitious."

"I may as well be. The company is already built. There is a generation of entrepreneurs returning to their roots, not only in Italy but across Europe and Asia. They want to go back to making things themselves. I want Di Rossi Textiles helping them."

On the way home, Lark again resumed her position on the train, looking out of her passenger window. This time, however, her headphones were left in her bag. Dario found an opening.

"So, Miss Chambers. What did you think?" Dario asked.

"Of... the show?"

"*Si.*"

"I... didn't know the difference between a knit and a woven, for starters."

"And now you know."

"And now I know."

"I noticed you couldn't help touching the brocades."

"Hmm... brocade. *Como si dice?*" she asked, in Italian, to indicate what she was after. *How do you say it?*

"*Broccato.*"

"*Broccato,*" she repeated, as though the word instantly joined the mass of her vocabulary. "The Indian fabrics?"

"*Si.* You love color, I think."

Lark shrugged. "Doesn't everyone?"

"Not everyone. And they are usually dressed the way you are now."

His jab garnered an unappreciative look.

"My job requires me to blend in to the background. The less you realize I'm there, the better I am at my job. Unfortunately, I wasn't able to give you a proper demonstration tonight."

"Tomorrow," he said.

"Indeed. Tomorrow."

"When you are alone you dress boldly," he dared to assume.

"Not really."

"Come now, *Allodola.* You may wish to pretend, but you cannot erase my memory. Your skin against every jewel tone that exists is the last sight I want to see before I die."

Lark's shoulders were shaking as he spoke.

"Why do you talk like that?" she said.

"How do I talk?"

"Like some... Italian rogue from a cheap, bawdy romance novel."

"You love it," he grinned provocatively in his thick accent. So provocatively, in fact, that she burst out laughing. He more than proved her point. His grin held.

Lark finally composed herself, shaking her head.

"I do," she dared confess, smiling. She looked at him with timid recollection, which left him further speechless, a distant spike in his heart rate.

This was going to be a long trip, he thought. He was suddenly glad to have gotten their inevitable dalliance out of the way early. Though he couldn't decide if their previous anonymity made it more sensual or less.

She broke her gaze from his and stared awkwardly into her lap while she reached into her bag in the seat next to her.

He fiddled with the cuff of his shirt, trying to get his smile to wane while Lark retreated back into whatever played between her earbuds, the click-clacking of the train filling in their pregnant silence.

7

Chapter 7

Early on as a child, Lark had a habit of mimicking people. She would hear something and compulsively repeat it, especially when it came to her teachers at school, her favorite place. Everything they said to the class had a certain sing song pattern and rhythm to it. She didn't even know that she was doing it.

Her first grade teacher hated it. The young teacher seemed to think Lark was making fun of her and she often got reprimanded.

But her Korean friends at the corner store found it endlessly amusing, the way Lark could mimic what she heard and repeat it flawlessly, saying things she had no idea she was saying.

Korean had been the first foreign language Lark had ever learned. She was six years old when her mother began leaving her alone for days at a time. She learned responsibility early, getting herself dressed and to school on time each morning, telling time by whatever cartoon was on. She would walk down to the corner store after school when she was bored, or when there was no food left in the house.

Right away Yumi, the elderly wife of the store owner, was

feeding her and teaching her words, pointing to everything that was in the store. Yumi had become a bit like a second mom until CPS picked her up, after her mother got arrested. The first time. When Lark took her Korean language exam in college, her professor marveled because she spoke like a native from her small village in Seoul.

For Lark, English and Korean were virtually interchangeable in her mind, and it took no effort to do the job Di Rossi Textiles was overpaying her to do. $600 bucks a day, not including her stipend, and she was jet setting to boot.

Yes, this was the therapy she needed after months of slogging through the mud and bowing under the burden of an entire country's dirty laundry. Perhaps it looked like running away, but she just needed a recharge. After awhile, whether she was sleeping underneath a tarp or sucking down caviar, it seemed she always had her suitcase ready, zipped and in the corner of her room. Ready to move on. "Going home" simply wasn't a thing. Ten years of foster care certainly taught her that.

The next morning after their trip to Milan, the trio met on the tarmac. Lark was dressed smartly in another crisp white shirt and a pencil skirt, this one navy. Her hair again pulled back. Dario wore his dress shirt with the sleeves rolled halfway up and beige linen pants. He surveyed her appearance that oddly seemed both flat and sharp at the same time.

"You do realize we will be travelling in a tube for several hours."

"That's one way of describing your private plane."

"You are dressed like a stewardess from the 80's."

Lark looked down at herself, evaluating her outfit.

"I have worn less comfortable clothes under far less convenient circumstances."

"Ah yes, I am aware of your time in Haiti. You have all afternoon to enlighten me."

Lark squinted in the direction of the still rising sunlight as the gentle wind blew stray wisps of her hair.

"Not something I'm ready to talk about, I'm afraid."

"Pity. Then it will be a long flight."

"You could tell me about yourself."

"That's something you would want to know?"

"Of course. Why wouldn't I?"

"You did not seem very interested the last time we were alone together."

His words forced her memory to their late night walk, their cramped, frenzied lovemaking in her extra long twin bed.

"Alone together? Yesterday, you mean? In front of the bathrooms?" she feigned ignorance.

"No..." he grinned, "but in fact you did not seem interested in talking to me then, either."

"Am I interrupting?" the senior Mr. Di Rossi approached them, grinning.

"Not at all, Signore De Rossi."

"You looked uncomfortable, signorina. You must excuse my son, he has a habit of being a bit blunt. He did not inherit any of my diplomacy."

"No, just your charm," Lark smiled. Dario looked at his old man.

Luca Di Rossi narrowed his eyes on Lark for a long time before grabbing her hand and kissing it. Lark smiled and laughed.

"If I were still a young man..." he began.

"But you are not," Dario filled in.

"Roberto, *bafangu chooch!*" he answered his son, along with an obscene Italian gesture. Lark continued to laugh. "Fuck yourself, jackass!" being what he essentially said.

Signore Di Rossi devoured much of Lark's attention on the way, saying the best way to practice his English is with a beautiful woman. Meanwhile, Dario listened as Lark politely engaged with his father, and he couldn't help but notice how poised and diplomatic she was as she maneuvered his embarrassing flirtations. In contrast, Dario also couldn't stop remembering the way she had begged to come on his cock. The memory flashed behind his eyes and sent a shudder through him.

It took some time, but one of his conquests had finally spilled over into his professional life. He'd supposedly walked out of hers, with a measly kiss that only he knew about.

The whole thing reminded him too much of the goodbye he'd given his own wife as she slipped away. He had been so relieved for the opportunity to say it, until it had passed. Then he was only bitter with anger. He should have never walked into that hospital room. He should have stayed out drinking wine all night after work, only to come back and find the room bare and clean. Then he wouldn't have had to accept the truth. He could've spent these last ten years in blissful denial.

At least Friday night showed him that it would have always happened the way that it did. He truly did prefer to say goodbye.

He welcomed the insight, morose as it made him.

After a half day of traveling they landed in Seoul, South Korea.

The city was bustling clean and modern, like an amusement park that never closed. The buildings loomed as large as any block of Broadway, and with just as much neon to rival it. They took a taxi to downtown Seoul where the modern, luxury hotel they were staying in was a sky high homage to old world Korean architecture. They approached the counter, eager to settle in.

"Excuse me, Mr. Di Rossi, but I only see a reservation for one penthouse suite."

"Check again. My assistant would have recently booked this."

"It looks like two rooms were booked, but they failed to secure the second room with a deposit, sir. The room was given away."

"But there should be three," Dario huffed, rubbing his forehead.

It'd been a long flight. Now, it was the day after the beginning of fashion week, and they'd have better luck knocking on doors than to find another hotel room in the city.

"*Que fato, Roberto?*" Signore Di Rossi inquired at the counter.

"There's been a mixup with the rooms, papa. Lenora must have messed up the reservations."

"*Allora*, what is our alternative?"

"The entire city is booked for fashion week, we have none."

"So we have no place to sleep?"

"Your suite was reserved. The other rooms, however were not."

"Sir, we have one cancellation we can give you," the concierge chimed in, "A single room on the third floor."

The senior Mr. Di Rossi wasted no time. "*Va bene.* I will take the room. The two of you will be sharing the suite."

"Signore, no!" Lark insisted, a bit too urgently. "Let me take the lesser room. Please."

"*Sciocchezza!* Enjoy yourself, Signora Chambers. Roberto. *Try not to make love to each other,*" Signor De Rossi urged them in Italian, relinquishing a sly smile. He found perverse enjoyment in Lark's stoic mask of panic. Dario returned his attention to the service counter.

"We'll take it," Dario replied.

* * *

They entered into a gorgeous suite with polished travertine floors, white furniture and masculine accents of dark mahogany wood. The suite took up the whole floor and had two rooms at opposite ends, each bedroom sleek, modern and overlooking the Seoul skyline.

"This is too much," Lark commented. "It's far too... luxurious."

"It is a luxury hotel, *Allodola*. This is the only way they come."

"But this is... clearly for an owner of a renown textile company," Lark went on, "your father should share this suite with you, not me."

Dario found her sentiment amusing.

"Fortunately, my father values our relationship over luxury. As do I. And the two of us sharing a room would ruin it," he assured her. "Relax, *cara*. Everyone is happy. Especially me."

"You're not going to be a problem, are you Mr. Di Rossi?"

A bolt of arousal hit him at her words. So dutiful. The differences between Lark and Vanessa were like night and day.

"Certainly not," he insisted. "I do not make a habit of seducing women."

"You don't?"

"No. Especially women who work for me."

"Then I am especially safe, according to you."

"*Certo*."

"Good."

"But... most of the women who work for me are relatives. And, I do occasionally enjoy the challenge of turning on a woman without touching her."

She was sure it was a joke until his green eyes met hers, veiled as if for her protection.

"*Che cazzo*, how does that help me!" she exclaimed. He only smiled.

"It doesn't. Ladies first," he gestured, urging her to pick a room. They were identical, so she went left. He went right, watching her close the bedroom door behind her.

* * *

They only had a half hour to check in and freshen up before they were on the move again. Instantly they were in meetings with a young local designer gearing up for his fashion week slot.

"Signore Di Rossi, it's an honor," the young designer said through Lark, their interpreter, with genuine awe.

His name was Park Tae-hwan, creator of a burgeoning Korean brand called SALVA.

"Thank you for hosting us," the senior Mr. Di Rossi said in Italian, per Lark's request. She wanted the challenge, she'd said. And to earn her keep.

"We've had many brands scout Korea as a location. Gucci, Louis Vuitton, Versace. The young people here are hungry for any and all things Western culture, especially streetwear."

"I'm afraid streetwear is not our specialty," Signore Di Rossi continued, "but we have relationships with every major Italian brand."

"I know, I've done the research. I'm pleased that Di Rossi Textiles has considered catering more to the youth market. Korea has been a rich country for many years now, several successful conglomerates have made the country very prosperous, especially the city of Seoul. Lots of disposable income."

"The numbers make sense, but we are curious: why is competition so low in such a thriving market?" Dario asked.

"Unfortunately, none of the notable brands that scout here

follow through with choosing Seoul as a location."

"Is it the growing competition by counterfeit merchants?"

Park seemed impressed by Dario's research as he answered.

"It plays a factor, but the main reason is a bit complex," he replied as the men walked. "Korea is a very... homogenous culture. We don't get an interior influx of perspectives the way it is in America and Europe. It causes a very strict social hierarchy to form, a compulsive sense of conformity."

"I don't understand," Signore Di Rossi furrowed his brow. "Fashion is about setting trends, no? It sounds like the perfect place for a fashion house to set up shop."

"It is. Until the trend becomes something else."

"You're saying Korean fashion values trends to a fault?" Dario asked.

"Precisely," Park nodded. "It is simply too volatile for an established brand to set up a permanent place here."

"Korea is where innovation comes to die?"

Park laughed. "That is a bit harsh perhaps, but yes. New designers are at a disadvantage abroad, and unfortunately even more so at home."

"Forgive me, it was a joke," Dario stopped to give a light bowing gesture of diplomacy. "You will grow accustomed to my sense of humor."

"Well, it certainly did not lose itself in translation. Your interpreter is exquisite," Lark heard herself say.

She smiled, fading further into the background as she lowered her head, mimicking the respectful leanings of the culture itself. So she didn't notice Dario looking over at her with a slight grin.

"I don't speak Korean, but if it is anything like her Italian, I am sure it *is* exquisite," she reddened as she interpreted his words.

"That doesn't surprise me in the least," Park said, looking over at Lark.

He conducted a private conversation with her for a bit. She loosened, politely answering his questions but eager to once again disappear, as if breaking character in the midst of a play.

The men continued to talk business and Lark was their seamless, invisible telephone in the ear of each man, talking quietly and on a delay behind what the other party said.

They took a tour through the young designer's workroom and retail space before leaving, agreeing to convene the following day at tomorrow's runway show, bright and early. Then, Lark would have the night off.

They returned to the hotel with plenty of the evening left.

"What are your plans, *Allodola?*" he struck up conversation in the elevator.

"None tonight. Except to cruise the Korean market. I may go and see... an old friend before we leave here."

"An old friend?"

"Yes. Family, really. Family of family."

Lark still kept in touch with Yumi, who told her where to go and to stay with her relatives there.

"Is this 'family' how you came to learn Korean?" Dario asked.

"More or less."

"Do you have a favorite language?"

"Depends on my mood."

"And what is your mood today?"

"Today? *It's Korean,*" she replied in the native tongue. She couldn't wait to get to the street market and taste hot fresh Korean meat from a cart, dripping with sauce and laying on beds of rice and sprouts and fresh noodles.

They got to the penthouse suite and he opted for the plush

living room couch rather than the privacy of his own room. She couldn't resist an opportunity to be near him, especially one not related to work, even though her frenzied desire was molten underneath her thin- yet sturdy- professional veneer.

Lark kicked off her shoes, strategically choosing a bar stool off the kitchen island area a polite distance away.

"May I join you tonight?" he inquired.

She was startled by the ask. She didn't want to be rude. She didn't *not* want him to go. She didn't know what she wanted, or how to say it.

"Tonight? I... of course."

"We have a long day tomorrow and I'd like to see more of the city. With you."

Lark stuttered.

"Signore Di Rossi is welcome to come as well," she offered.

"Come now, *Allodola.* I am as professional as you are," he chastised her.

"I didn't mean to imply—"

"Unless... you are afraid of yourself?" he asked with an alluring stare, one that seemed to be native to Italian men.

Lark intentionally ignored him, though her brain skipped a few beats. "Doesn't your father like Korean food?"

"He does, but if I may be honest, this is more time than we have spent together in many years."

"Ah. You could use the break," she replied.

"I'm glad you understand."

"You may be interested in a break from me once we're done," she ventured, trying not to sound obvious.

"I highly doubt that," he assured. "Give me an hour to change."

Lark rolled her eyes. "Honestly. Y'all are worse than American women."

"Y'all?" he teased her.

"Italian men," she grinned, amused at her own grammatical slip-up. She was so jet-lagged, she was surprised she hadn't completely shed her professional dialect. She let out a sigh.

"Fine, I'll wait. I've only been dreaming about it since we landed, what's another hour?"

When they left, Lark too had changed, but only into a flattering pair of jeans, her plain white dress shirt still on as well as her heels. Dario had to eat his earlier words. She could be stylish when she wanted to.

She relied too heavily on the fundamentals, he theorized as they got in the elevator, out into the night air from the lobby. Mixing and matching the basics among themselves was a hopeless snoozefest, no matter how chic the pieces. He had plans for young Lark. When he looked at her it made him think of silk chiffon.

The colorful Korean street signs put Time's Square to shame, stacked up to the sky yet hanging low enough to almost reach out and touch. The vertical Korean script illuminated the tall buildings that lined the street market alley.

The smells were intoxicating. Lark insisted on trying a little of everything, and Dario played along, not allowing her to use a penny of the stipend they'd given her. They split a steamed roll filled with myriad meat and vegetables as they found a place to sit next to each other on a sidewalk bench among the bustling natives.

"Truly, I must tell you, *Allodola*, you surprise me," he began.

"How's that?"

"On paper, your credentials are very impressive. But it is another thing to see your mastery in person."

"Thank you, signore."

"I tried not to let my astonishment show. I have immense respect for the amount of expertise and concentration you've poured into your work. It is a special person that can excel in a field that functions optimally when it is the least noticeable."

That tongue. His flattery and compliments were like a spell. He somehow knew how to zero in on the thing you most wanted to hear from another human. No wonder their company had almost no turnover rate, right down to the janitorial staff. Even if he hadn't been a Di Rossi, he would've made it straight to the top.

"You embarrass me, Mr. Di Rossi."

"Call me Dario. You are not working now."

"Okay. Dario. I must compliment your English as well."

"You patronize me, signora," he grinned, showing off his exquisite looks. His jawline looked as though it was drawn, even under his 5 o'clock shadow. His eyes had one setting: devour. It made men fall in line and it made women positively helpless.

"I wouldn't hesitate to correct your English if it needed correcting, signore. You sound as though you've been taught by Italian teachers is all. Your vocabulary is superior to most Americans."

"I do not always understand Americans. They are worse than Sicilians."

"Indeed," Lark chuckled. "We... have many dialects."

"Don't you mean 'ya'll'?"

"I'm never going to hear the end of that," she sighed. He laughed a bit, sitting back in his place on the bench.

"Do you come from a family of dialects?" he delved.

"I don't come from a family at all," she confessed.

"No? You are an orphan?" he asked in a curious tone.

"Essentially. I was in foster homes until I was 18."

She didn't think she would ever bring this up at work, and here they were speaking of it on her first day, practically. Thankfully, he didn't give her the pity stare.

"Ah. You met many people, and learned many languages," he filled in the gaps.

"*Si.*"

"Italian was your first new language," he guessed.

She shook her head. "Korean."

"Hm. Your foster family?"

"The grocery store owner, in the building where my mother lived. Before I was taken."

"Did they not take you in?"

"...They tried," Lark didn't elaborate.

"Do you keep in contact with your mother?" he wondered.

Lark thought about the last time she saw her. Re-married and with a young daughter of four, her half sister. Still a drunk, still picking losers to shack up with. She'd recently called to say she thought it best that they keep their relationship distant for the sake of her "family." Lark expected any day to get the same call her relatives must've gotten, asking to take in her half sister as well.

"Very little. I hardly know her."

"What about your father?"

"Forgive me, Mis... Dario," she said, remaining professional, "this isn't a pleasant topic for me."

"*Ma dai*, Haiti, your former lover, your childhood. Everything about you is unfit for conversation."

"Now you're getting it," she smiled.

"This is the past you referred to? The one you plan to outrun?"

It took a moment for Lark to recall their conversation on the street, where she admitted to trying to outrun the past, and he the future.

"Very good memory, signore," she said without confirming or denying.

"Dario," he corrected her again. *"Va bene*, tell me how you learned Italian."

"I always wanted to. So I did. Italian was my fourth language."

"How old were you?"

"Fourteen."

"Mama mia," he said in perfect stereotypical fashion. She laughed.

"What draws you to Italia?"

She smiled as though he'd outed her.

"Is it so obvious?"

He simply nodded.

She thought about it, feeling naked as she spoke. "I don't know. Everything about it is beauty, and love of it. It's in everything. Even in the dullest parts of society."

"Beauty," he sat back, studying her. "Are you sure this is the word you are looking for?"

She gave him a shy turn of her head.

"I sense you believe that you already know the answer to this question you've asked."

"Si," he said, nursing his food. "The word you are looking for is 'passion.'"

"Ah," she nodded her head, smiling, as if having an epiphany.

"Would you care to be enlightened?" he asked as he sat back arrogantly. She laughed.

"Please."

"We have many Africans in Italy," he said.

Uh oh.

Lark braced herself for a bizarre exchange.

"They too are a passionate people. Creative," he said, looking intently at her as he pointed. "You were born in a country created by Brits descended from Germans. The sticks in the mud of Europe. You are starving."

She laughed.

"*Ma dai*," she mimicked him, "then why wouldn't I just go to Africa?"

"*Because* you were born in a country created by Brits descended from Germans. Europe is your father. Look at you."

"What about me?"

"You are dressed like a boy from Dickens," he said. She laughed as he continued. "You must drown your beautiful brown skin in color. How do you not know this?"

"I can't very well wear a gold wrap dress to work."

"Why the hell not? We are an Italian textile company."

"I'm not auditioning to be a model, I'm here to be your voice."

"Italian men like to gaze on beauty. Your boring blouse is making my dick sad."

"Good," she said after rolling her eyes. Workplace harassment still had many years to go in Italy, it seemed. But then, it was part of the reason she came.

"What about France?" she argued.

"What *about* Francia?"

"They're not sticks in the mud. And they had a hand in our little national experiment."

"A hand? They just use treaties as an excuse to fuck everyone... *como si dice... indiscriminante.*"

Lark cackled. "Indiscriminately, yes. And taught us how to make roux."

"*Oui.*"

"And thus, I was born," Lark said with a pinky in the air.

"You are part French?"

"Distantly. So I've been told," she answered, chewing.

"*Madonna*, no wonder you fuck the way you do," he daringly replied.

His words pumped throbbing arousal through her that rendered her speechless. They *had* fucked, hadn't they? For a nanosecond she'd nearly forgotten. Her cheeks warmed and she wiped her mouth with a napkin to stall. He was testing her, perhaps. She was determined to pass.

"I'm sure I have no idea what you mean by that," she offered an amused yet reprimanding glance. He huffed a laugh.

"So this is your plan? Never to talk about it?"

"That is precisely my plan, Mr. Di Rossi."

"Dario."

"That is precisely my plan, Dario."

"You cannot avoid your mistakes forever, *Allodola*."

Lark stiffened.

Mistakes?

She kept a calm visage as his choice of words stabbed at her ruthlessly. Outwardly she smiled.

"Have we met?" Lark finally said with a raised eyebrow. He laughed again in response.

8

Chapter 8

After another long day of meetings, Dario was again sharing his suite with Lark, enjoying another evening of room service.

"Do you know what you will do after your time here?"

"The agency has found me an assignment at the Embassy in Qatar."

"That sounds exciting."

"It is. It'll be nice to brush up on my Arabic."

"And after that?"

Lark looked at him as though the thought hadn't occurred to her.

"Don't know. I was supposed to be going on vacation when I took this job. Perhaps I will. Or maybe I'll go back to the U.N. and beg them for my old job back."

"Is that what you want?"

Lark took a deep breath as she pondered the question.

"Eventually I'd like something a little more... stable. Permanent."

"That surprises me."

"I don't strike you as the stable type?"

"Honestly, no."

"No?"

"You certainly have the dress code down, but you do not like to be confined."

Lark smiled as she shrugged.

"I suppose I suffer from boring too easily. So much traveling and I become bored with that too."

It was the only time they had a chance to get acquainted. Normally Dario despised small talk, and it seemed so did Lark, who often retreated to her headphones in between meetings, leaving his insufferable father as his only chatting companion.

He was beginning to wonder if she even had anything playing at all, as if she merely had no other way to politely tell her bosses to fuck off while she wasn't working. He imagined the mental energy it took to interpret between two non-native languages required one to recharge when off the clock.

As much as he understood, part of him wanted to make Lark swoon the way Vanessa had on the night they met, which she couldn't do when they weren't talking. At least, not without sacrificing their burgeoning professional rapport.

They had two days left in Korea before heading to New York, and he hadn't anticipated the amount of downtime he would have. They were at meetings and shows eight hours a day, four hours less than his average workday. He didn't know what to do with himself and was about to do something drastic. Like, indulge his appetites.

The instantaneous chemistry they'd experienced only a week before was still having its way with his warring libido. The salted caramel of her skin. If he tried hard enough— and he had— he could still feel the way her thighs had gripped him, the way they had filled her cozy bedroom with the damp heat of lovemaking.

He lay in bed mulling over his blunder the other night, the moment he'd referred to their affair as a "mistake."

He regretted the existence of his mouth as soon as he heard himself. Her energy had completely changed and an awkward silence enveloped them both.

Obviously, he hadn't regretted anything, but he assumed from her complete unwillingness to talk about it that she had deemed it a mistake.

But he assumed wrong.

He wasn't sure what it meant, but whatever it was, his stupid mouth had rendered it irrelevant.

Now he was sequestered in his room, pretending to be asleep.

He wanted to clear the air, but professionally speaking he couldn't deny that the misunderstanding might be what he needed to make it through this trip.

If he let her think that he regarded her rendezvous with him a mistake, then she wouldn't think anything of it if he were to get up and knock on her door right now.

She would think he was jet-lagged, perhaps a little self-absorbed, and growing a newfound interest in talking to her about random things not related to business. And all of those things were true.

He emerged from his room, traversing the great crevasse between her side and his, to Lark's door. Dario hesitated a moment, took a deep breath, and then knocked.

* * *

The sudden knock on the door made Lark nearly jump out of her skin.

86

She was completely naked under her robe, and even though her door was locked and there was no danger of him seeing her, her heart was beating a mile a minute. She dressed herself in a panic, grabbing a t-shirt and a pair of sweats.

Her Russian audio droned on in the background as she opened the door. There she was confronted with Dario, wearing head to toe cashmere and barefoot. His brown tufts of hair were a bit wet and curly at the ends as though from a shower.

"Am I interrupting?"

She shook her head and opened the door further for him to enter.

He looked around, her room kept and neat as though room service also slept there.

"Can't sleep?" she offered.

"No," he shook his head.

She resumed her cross-legged position on the turned-down bed, a spiral notebook and a box of unidentifiable Korean treats in front of her.

"Jet lag, I suppose," she babbled, mesmerized by the look of him, his cream-colored shirt that draped his broad back.

He sat at one of the two leather chairs and table in the corner with his long legs stretched in front of him, a faint musky scent filling her room.

He was so damn elegant. The way Landon, her former boss at the U.N. had been to her. She swooned like the naive young recruit that she was, and here she was back in that same position, like deja vu. Only Dario was wickedly more handsome, to the point that it filled all her senses. He had the alpha-male gait, commanded every room he walked in like other men of a certain age and stature. No one could blame her for repeating history.

"Is this what you listen to? In your headphones?" he asked.

"Yes," she grinned, pleased that he noticed.

"How do you keep them all straight? In your head?"

She knew he meant the languages.

"I can keep them straight," she said, "the difficult part is keeping them all fresh when I'm not using them."

"Hence the Russian audio."

"Da."

"So you are always working."

"Not unlike yourself."

"*Si*, but don't you ever want to take a break?"

"I didn't always do this," she informed him. "I had to learn. When I had a new assignment I would cram and cram for hours the night before my first day and I'd be exhausted. It's much easier to keep up an hour a night regimen."

"You are very self-disciplined."

"I'm in a penthouse suite overlooking the South Korean skyline. The least I could do is be self-disciplined."

"I want to hear them all."

"All the languages?" she smiled.

"*Si*. How many do you know?"

"Well, technically I speak eleven languages, but I have only have certified mastery in seven. Soon to be eight."

"Frankly, I don't believe you," he said. She laughed.

"Well, you've heard the English, the Italian, the Korean," she counted on her fingers.

"A bit of the French," he said.

"*Oui...*" she said. "So...there's Arabic."

She switched between the remaining languages as though switching through split personalities. He smiled.

"You're a fascinating woman," he said, as if trying to use his tongue on her the only way that was still allowed.

"As are you, signore."

"I am a fascinating woman?" he made a corny joke. Politely she laughed.

They stayed up far too late, he maintaining his distance at the sitting area, she in bed. They ordered room service again, and she taught him many words.

"It's better to use some kind of trick or shorthand and use that as a... hm... what's the word," she said. He looked at the indentation her breasts made through her shirt. He imagined seeing her topless again as she spoke.

"*Stele di Rosetta*," she said.

"*Si.* Rosetta Stone," he blinked, letting her know he understood.

"A picture or a feeling, the object itself, of course, if that applies."

"What if the word or phrase exists in one language but not another?"

Lark was impressed by his curiosity.

"That's... a very good question, signore."

"Dario," he corrected her again. "You musn't address a man of my stature so formally when he is in your room in the middle of the night. It's creepy," he said. She laughed, both at the insight and the very Italian way he said the word "creepy."

"Perhaps you will find this as fascinating as I do, since you asked that," she began, as she hiked her knee up and rested her chin there. "Whatever phrase I can't find in the English language, I can usually find it in ebonics."

"Ebonics?"

"African American slang."

"Ah. You have more than one slang."

"More like... the slang from which all other American slangs originate."

"The rosetta stone of slang," he said. She laughed.

"Well, perhaps we can't take credit for it all," she smiled. "But for instance. In Italian, in French, in practically every other language there is a verb tense for immediate actions. *Cosa stai fascendo*, what are you doing, right now, this very moment? See how many English words I had to use?"

"It is very taxing," he emphatically agreed. She laughed again.

"But in Ebonics, we have 'fixing' and it's incredibly useful. And if the verb is passive, we drop it. It's implied. Because without it, no one is confused and everyone knows *exactly* what the hell you're talking about, so guess what? Redundant."

"Like 'cosa' instead of 'che cosa,' or 'qual'. English uses 'what' for everything," he replied, to show he was following her.

"Exactly. So, the correct ebonics pronunciation of '*Cosa stai fascendo*' is 'What you fixin' to do' or, even more precisely, 'What you finna do?'"

"Whaachufinnadoo," he said.

Lark fell over into her pillows and practically died at his pronunciation of ebonics.

So he said it again. Lark laughed until she couldn't breathe.

"*Ma dai*, he exclaimed with his hands out like an Italian mafia movie boss. "I am saying it perfect."

Lark could only nod.

"That's why it's so funny," she finally said when she'd fully recovered. He smiled.

Lark was suddenly glad to know that he'd considered their night together a mistake. In light of the fact that he was long widowed, she perceived herself a welcome distraction for him at the very least, just as she was now. Their professional relationship was something separate and seemed to be progressing nicely, nice enough that they could sleep in the same suite together without a problem. Whatever loss of respect or mystery she may have suffered, it inadvertently caused her to become more unguarded and friendly than she thought she could manage. He eyed her playfully.

"Whachufinnadoo," he said again for effect, the pronunciation already improving.

"Please stop!" she yelled into her pillow. He relinquished an unbearably sexy laugh, delighted at the sight of her.

* * *

The last day of fashion week, the trio returned to the hotel ready to crash.

"Roberto, I am beginning to wonder what this trip accomplishes," the senior Mr. Di Rossi complained.

"Just know that it will make us money in the long run, papa."

"I hope so. Every day I am parched from so much talking."

"A usual day for you, no?"

"*Bafangu.* You do not appreciate me."

"Not true. The two of us accomplish much more than we do alone. The Koreans are polite, is all. You must have patience."

"*Allodola*, what do you think?" the senior Mr. Di Rossi turned to Lark, taking his son's cue and using the Italian version of her name. Dario staved off annoyance.

"If I were doing business with you, I would be very impressed," Lark said with a glance to her other boss.

Lark suspected his question was only an excuse for him to take her hand again and kiss it, which he did. She giggled.

"*Va bene*, Roberto wake me when it is tomorrow," he said,

entering an open elevator. Lark and Dario stood waiting for the penthouse.

"Last one upstairs has to pay for room service," she said.

"Actually I have an... engagement."

"Oh. I see," Lark replied, oblivious.

"Order anything you want and charge it to the room."

"Technically, I have an engagement of my own."

"Ah. To see your family?"

"*Si.* You remembered."

"Of course," he said as the elevator doors opened. Lark entered alone.

"*Va bene.* My father will be available, of course, if you need anything."

Lark had about as much desire to let the senior Di Rossi talk her ear off as Dario did.

"Thank you, Mr. Di Rossi," she said, as the doors closed. Dario didn't correct her formal address. He turned to make his way out of the lobby.

Upstairs, Lark freshened up, changed only out of her pumps and into flats, and headed to Yumi's sister's.

She'd purposely waited the last night of the trip, in case she needed to excuse herself politely and quickly. She hadn't expected more than a formal greeting.

But Yumi's sister opened up her home to her.

Turns out she'd heard much about Lark from Yumi, ever since she was a young girl coming into the store and learning words. Lark greeted her fondly. She met uncles, cousins, siblings, wives, and infants. They exchanged phones full of pictures and Lark did her best to describe New York, where Yumi still lived over bowls of bulgogi and homemade kimchi.

The sense of family was overwhelming, and she couldn't wait

to get out of there. She politely excused herself as she expected, taking a taxi back to downtown Seoul.

When she got back to the hotel it was dark. She peeked into the restaurant, which was slow, even for a Sunday evening. She took a seat at the bar in the corner, perusing the menu, but she was craving something, in particular, that wasn't on it.

She thought perhaps she could earn herself some brownie points with the chef.

"Ready to order, ma'am?" the bartender asked her politely in English.

"*I don't suppose the chef could go through the trouble of making me a burger,*" Lark asked in her politest Korean. The bartender smiled.

"*Say no more,*" he replied, bowing. Jackpot.

Just as she was finishing the life-changing burger at the hotel bar, she spotted Dario with a beautiful dark haired Korean woman, sitting at a table, gazing at each other as though they were in love.

She froze, suddenly trying to shrink herself and make herself unrecognizable as she sat at the bar. Her heartbeat skyrocketed as though she were witnessing a murder.

In a way, she was. It was the image of himself that he was killing. One of the long-suffering widower that his father had painted. Though widowers were men too and had to get it somehow.

Only Dario seemed like a true romantic. Even with the little she knew of him. Not a wealthy playboy.

Perhaps she *was* the one who had ended his drought?

Not likely.

In fact, it was much more likely she was another link in a long chain of rendezvous. Secret ones, if his father's side of the story was any indication. Maybe he was once a devoted husband and father, but it'd only been a week since their own weekend fling and he was on to the next. That man was long gone, it would seem.

Oh well. At least she knew her instincts were right. He may have turned out to be her boss, but he was indeed trouble, as she suspected.

She had a sliver of burger left that suddenly she couldn't seem to finish.

Her body in her barstool was like cement, until she saw from the mirrored partition behind the bar that Dario excused himself to get up from the table, and out into the lobby. Then she made her move.

He was nowhere to be seen, so he must be in the men's room, she thought. She swiftly made her way across the lobby to the elevators, afraid to look back in case he was behind her, watching.

She stood behind the lobby wall, peeked around the corner, and didn't have to wait long to see Dario emerge from the men's room and back into the hotel restaurant.

Lark's breath caught in her throat. She didn't release it until she heard the elevator doors open, retreating safely inside.

What on Earth was wrong with men, she thought as she sighed and rolled her eyes.

He couldn't at least wait until they were in New York in a day? Fashion week was months away there. There were plenty of hotels, plenty of women. Plenty of other places to fuck rather than the penthouse suite that he just *haaad* to share with his interpreter.

Was he really going to force her to stay up all night, trying not to pretend to not be hearing things emanating from his room?

Tomorrow, they were going to have to have a talk.

That night she let the pity she felt for herself keep her awake far too long. She stroked the luxurious pillows and propped one up sideways next to her, roughly the size of a men's head, shoulders, and torso but nothing of the proportion, let alone the weight. She sighed as she skimmed her hand across the fabric of the pillowcase, the 1500 thread count betwixt her fingers.

She fell for his... everything. The way that other young woman seemed to. And why not? He talked a good game. She had been grateful. She still had no regrets, even now. Whether he considered the whole experience a "mistake" or not. She scoffed, thinking about his Korean companion again. *Was she in for one hell of an evening,* Lark thought.

The next morning, she emerged from her room and stood by the door, packed and ready for the airport. Minutes later, Dario also emerged from his room as though he'd been in it all night. He was clean-shaven, which made him look younger by at least a decade, and freshly pressed with the focused look of a gorgeous, angelic machine.

"*Pronto?*" he said.

"Just waiting for you," she replied. They abandoned the now empty room and entered the elevators. She watched him stifle a yawn as they descended.

"Tired?" Lark raised an eyebrow.

"*Si.*"

Don't bring it up, don't bring it up.

"You and your date must've... overexerted yourselves last night."

"'Date?'" Dario seemed oblivious.

"I saw the two of you. At the restaurant. I was at the bar," she outed him.

95

Dario looked ahead, his eyes shifting as though he were embarrassed, apologetic.

"That was not... a date."

Lark's eyebrows went up in surprise.

Dario Di Rossi liked to pay for it, apparently.

"I see..."

"Is what I do in my personal time a problem for you, Miss Chambers?" he politely asked.

"Certainly not, signore."

"Our professional relationship flows two ways, *vero*?"

"I couldn't agree more, signore. In fact, I think from now on, that's how it should remain."

"Meaning?"

"Meaning, no more sharing rooms, no more late-night chatter, no more room service. I pay my own way, I only work during business hours, and anything beyond that is overtime. We'll address each other formally, same as any other assignment. I won't take advantage of your kindness, and I'll expect you to not take advantage of mine."

"Very well."

"Good."

The elevator let off a chime for each floor they passed on their descent.

"I would appreciate it if you kept what you saw between us, signora."

"If you wish, Mr. Di Rossi."

"I don't like family or colleagues knowing about my... private life."

"Of course, signore."

There was another beat of silence, as the elevator seemed to be taking the long way down. Dario's eyes went skyward.

"You were not supposed to see that," he sighed.

The elevator ding indicating their arrival to the lobby inter-rupted them. The doors smoothly opened and Lark simply extended the long arm of her small suitcase as she exited the elevator car, pretending not to hear his final sentiment.

9

Chapter 9

A day later they were in New York, their bodies a full fourteen hours behind. They took a cab ride in silence to the Waldorf Astoria in the city, exhausted from travel. Luckily, this time the reservations were correct. But they were each on separate floors.

"Miss Chambers, I'll need you to accompany me for a meeting. Wait for my call."

"Of course, Mr. Di Rossi," she answered cordially as the elevator doors closed.

An hour later, she was in front of concierge waiting for him to emerge from the elevators. When he finally he did, he had changed into a gorgeous light brown suit, looking every inch the wealthy Italian businessman, or possible celebrity.

Lark found herself gawking shamelessly as he entered the lobby. He garnered looks this way and that from random passers-by, walking past them oblivious as their eyes continued to follow his path.

She knew what they were thinking: who is that, and where the fuck was he going? And they were jealous of whatever that place was.

It was a feeling she knew well because she'd felt it every day for ten days now. And every day she would answer the question.

Wherever he is going, he is taking you with him.

And just as it did every day, her heart skipped a beat at the thought, only it was more intense since they had agreed to keep their relationship as professional as possible.

His eyes met hers while she was lost in thought and it caught her off guard, giving her stomach a jolt. He gave her a teasing glare as they got close, one as playful as it was familiar.

"*Andiamo*, Stewardess Chambers," he said, teasing her about her wardrobe.

She felt the jealous stares gather intensity like a spotlight. She grinned. When he kept walking, she followed behind.

"Will Signore Di Rossi be joining us?"

"Not this time," he said as they exited through the oversized revolving door.

Lark stopped in her tracks on the large sidewalk as he hailed a cab. She was looking forward to never having to be alone with him again on this trip.

But it just so happened that the two of them needed to go to top-secret meetings? In America?

The traffic suffered a hiccup as if the cab drivers were falling all over themselves to pick him up. He noticed Lark was a ways behind him.

"What?" he said.

"Where are we going?" she asked.

"To a meeting."

"Really."

"Of course," he furrowed his brow as he opened the taxi door, gesturing for her to get in. She did, somewhat exasperated.

"27th and 8th," he told the driver as he shut the door. And they were off. She looked out her window at the city, not facing him.

"What is it, now?" he guessed at her mood, looking at the drive ahead.

"What a waste of money, Dario," she replied, shaking her head.

"Tell me how you really feel, Miss Chambers."

"What use am I in New York anyway?"

"I happen to be meeting with some Russian clients, and I'm going to need your help."

"I see. Does Signore Di Rossi even know about this meeting?"

"...Not yet."

Lark turned her head slightly, giving him a glare through the side of her almond shaped eyes.

"What've you got up your sleeve, Dario?"

"You are on company time, Miss Chambers," he said with a short tone, giving her a stern look that made her hot all over.

She felt her armpits spark with heat, she started to sweat. She'd overstepped their professional boundary that she staunchly insisted on, and he'd noticed.

"I was hired by Signore Di Rossi, was I not?" she dared reply, implying that perhaps he was not entirely the boss of her.

"You were not."

Lark faced forward, looking straight ahead for a moment, her eyes darted absentmindedly while she sat quietly.

If the senior Mr. Di Rossi hadn't hired her, it meant that Dario had. He'd seen her qualifications and chosen her himself, requested her himself.

"What does Signore Di Rossi *do*, exactly?" she shrugged.

"These days? Not much."

"He must be bored to tears on this trip."

"No. All he has ever wanted was to brush shoulders and tell his stories. And occasionally flirt. He is living the dream."

"You sound a bit bitter."

"Perhaps," he sighed. "I inherited quite the mess. But he has maintained our reputation. People recognize his face, not mine."

"Do these clients know he will not be at the meeting?"

"They will," he replied.

"These potential 'Russian' clients," Lark piped up again. "Are they... from the mafia or something?"

"Of course not."

"Signore Di Rossi doesn't care what goes on in his own company?"

"It is not his company, it is his great grandfather's, and soon it will be mine. You have turned very inquisitive, Miss Chambers," he stoically replied.

She stiffened as she quickly answered back, "Not at all, I'm just wondering why we had to come all the way here. We were much closer to Russia."

"Because they are here," he replied just as quickly. "Had we actually flown to Russia, then you should be worried."

She was quiet for a moment, likely thinking of another rebuttal, he presumed. He was right.

"Surely, they speak English," she said.

He stifled a smile as he looked out of the window, the bumpy cab ride tossing them about like a horse-drawn carriage.

"*Si.* But... it is our first meeting, and I don't want to give too much away. Besides, we have a reputation to maintain. It is a convenience we can afford."

"You want me to interpret Russian into Italian?"

"Yes, Miss Chambers, will that be a problem?"

"No, *Mr. Di Rossi*. I just wish I had a head's up," Lark replied in a huff.

"Are you angry with me?" he asked.

"Not at all."

"You seem... agitated."

It was true. She was agitated and she didn't entirely know why.

She hated the implication hanging over their conversation, that she was anything less than a consummate professional. He was the one fucking high paid prostitutes. And unsuspecting employees. On his own time, but still. How could *he* presume to correct her?

"I speak Russian, but I haven't mastered it," she replied instead, which wasn't a total lie. "I can do the job, I just... I don't like surprises is all."

"Make them speak English. I'll pretend I don't understand very well," he suggested.

Lark shook her head. "No. It's too big of a risk. Pretending you don't understand is much harder than you think."

"I'm sure you know aaaaaall about that, *cara mia*," he replied, as he stared out of the window, the backseat humming as they stopped at a red light. Lark let a smile escape as she nodded.

"I walked right into that one."

"*Si*," he grinned.

The cab made a stop at a vague location a block away from the Fashion Institute of Technology, which seemed to satisfy Dario. They got out and Lark quickly followed next to him as they entered a building, unmarked save for the address above the door in gold, the stone edifice covered in windows.

They got into an elevator and went straight to the top floor.

When the doors opened they went down a hallway and through a set of glass double doors, where a handful of men were waiting around a large oval table.

Sergei was young, blond and blue-eyed with his hair and gotee closely shaven. He had a scar across the side of his head where no hair could grow. He wore a vintage '80s U.S. Olympics tee underneath a blazer with jeans and stylish leather shoes. The men sitting with him were dangerous looking and non-descript, wearing black in various forms and shades.

Dario and Lark took seats across from them.

"Good afternoon, Mr. Di Rossi," one of the men began, presumably their interpreter, also quite young looking. It seemed Sergei and his lot were playing a similar game.

"Good afternoon. I can speak Russian as well— if you prefer to allow me the honor," Lark directed to him, "to save us all a bit of time."

The interpreter looked over to his boss, explaining in a surprised tone. Equally surprised, Sergei gave a raised eyebrow, then a nod of approval.

"Thank you for meeting with us Signore, when will your father be joining us?" Lark began in Sergei's words.

"I'm afraid he is detained," Dario answered.

"That is a shame. We were looking forward to meeting such a legend in the industry. I hope he didn't consider our meeting a nuisance."

"Not at all. He flew here especially, but something came up and could not be moved. Please, tell me more about your operation."

"Mine is an up and coming brand," Sergei explained. "Regulations make designing in Russia hard, but we want to remain there. We were considering moving our flagship office to Italy, just for the incentives. I would like to avoid that. Much of our brand revolves around mother Russia. I believe it would devastate the reputation we have built."

"How can we help?" Dario asked.

"It is hard to get Western brands in Russia. There are no duties on Italian fabrics, however. Especially textiles. We worked with Burberry in London and we nearly went belly up."

"I noticed that much of your... aesthetic seems to harken back to some very popular Italian trends."

"Yes, I'm feeling very inspired right now by...what is word? *Stilizatsiya?*

"*Si*, pastiche," Dario said.

"Your interpreter is very good," he said. Lark blushed as she interpreted the words, but kept her delivery forceful and bold to match his.

"We like to hire the best," Dario doted on her, without breaking his gaze with Sergei.

"I am wondering if she is from Moscow," he said, then turned his face toward her, as if expecting her to answer.

"*We were taught broadest accent possible, sir,*" she said in Russian.

"*Which is Moscow?*"

"*Which is Moscow.*"

"*Is your boss lying to us?*" he suddenly asked her.

Lark looked at Dario, who was already looking at her.

"*Don't look at him, look at me,*" Sergei said to her in Russian.

It took a moment for Lark to gain her bearings.

"*Nyet. This is Di Rossi's son. He is in charge now. His father is retired. Rubs shoulders. Nothing more,*" she said.

"*This you have seen?*"

"*Da.*"

"His son. He is boss?"

"Da," she said again. Dario once again watched her adopt the posture of a potted plant in the room. Sergei turned to him.

"Forgive my rudeness, Signore Di Rossi, it's just that we postponed our travel plans in order to coordinate this meeting. We want to make sure Di Rossi Textiles is taking us seriously."

"I hope my interpreter has convinced you that is the case."

"She has."

"Very good."

"I would like for you to meet my distributor, who is also here in town for one day only. Tomorrow. Do you think Signore Di Rossi will be able to attend?"

"It is short notice, but I will try my best to make it happen."

"Please do. My distributor is a great admirer. My assistant will give you the details."

The pair of them were wordless until they were in a cab and on their way back to the hotel. Lark was the first to break the silence, with raised eyebrows.

"So...that was weird," she stated the obvious.

"What did he say?" he asked, betraying no sense of urgency. He didn't seem to be worried, so she didn't know how to feel.

"He just wanted to know if you were lying to him," she said.

"And?"

"Of course, I told him 'no.'"

"'Nyet,' yes I that part I heard. What else did you say?"

"I... may have had to throw your father under the bus a bit. I used a little of our prior conversation to convince him that you were the brains behind it all. I'm sorry, Mr. Di Rossi, he caught me off guard."

"No need. You did the right thing."

"So, what the hell's going on?" Lark insisted.

Dario figured she earned the right to know.

"I think... he might be in the counterfeit business," he divulged.

"Why on Earth are you meeting with criminals?" she asked, sounding galled.

"I am only speculating," he answered, guardedly. "Obviously he would not tell me such a thing outright, which I appreciate. He spends a lot of money on fabrics. Much of that is heavily taxed. He could spend a fortune with us, and also make a fortune."

"And you want his business."

"I do. But, for now, it is only a suspicion."

Lark was quiet for the moment, looking out the window. This cab ride was much smoother.

"Could you be implicated? Legally?" she asked.

"We would not, but it would obviously blemish the Di Rossi name, somewhat," he answered truthfully.

"And if he is truly a designer?"

"Then it would bring De Rossi into the 21st century. Youth combined with tradition, trendy combined with quality."

"This is your vision."

"*Si.*"

"But it's not your father's," Lark guessed.

"My father has no vision, except 'do not be the one that tanks the Di Rossi fortune.'"

"Has he succeeded?"

"Barely. But he is in no way cut out for this. So in that sense, I hold a deep respect for him."

In a much shorter span of time, they were back in front of the hotel.

"So what's next?" Lark asked as they made their way back inside.

"Next, we meet with this 'distributor' of his. We will see what happens."

That evening, Signore Di Rossi invited the two of them to dinner in the hotel's steakhouse, where he ordered a massive steak.

"*Belissimo*," he said when it arrived, "It's not Italy but it will do. The Korean food did not agree with me."

"May I try a piece, Signore?" Lark asked, sitting next to him.

"Please, Signora Chambers, take my meat," the elder Di Rossi pointedly insisted. Lark laughed with a shake of her head, cutting herself a carmelized section of meat. The two men exchanged looks.

"I love a woman who eats red meat."

"Miss Chambers will never work for us again, papa."

"Roberto, let me have my fun. When you are an old man you will understand."

"The two of you are adorable," she said. Dario's father reached over and grabbed him by the neck, kissing his forehead while Dario looked unamused.

"We are near your old stomping grounds, *Allodola*, no?"

Dario's jaw clenched. His father's use of the nickname was even more annoying now that he was barred from using it.

"*Si*," she replied, "within walking distance, in fact."

"This is my seventh trip to Nuova York, and I have never stayed at the Waldorf."

"You should've ordered the salad, signore."

"Would you like one?"

"I've had it, signore," she grinned.

"Have you tasted the Italian food here?"

"You mean... in New York?"

"*Certo.*"

LOVE ON A LARK

"Yes, signore," Lark giggled.

"So heavy! We must eat before we leave."

"Couldn't agree more, signore."

"'Signore, signore.' We are not in the military Miss Chambers. *E in Italiano, per favore.* I want to hear more of my language out of your beautiful mouth as I eat," he said, inhaling a bloody piece of his porterhouse.

"*Very well, but it will cost you double,*" she complied, smiling. The senior Mr. Di Rossi laughed.

"You speak Italian like you were born to it. *Are you Italian at heart?*" he asked in Italian.

"*Si,*" she laughed.

"Talk to me," he pleaded.

"*What shall I say?*" she replied, her intonation so precise that it elicited a snicker from Dario.

"Answer the question. Honestly," Signore Di Rossi, insisted.

She assessed that he was probably quite the Casanova back in the day. He didn't have the commanding presence of his son, but he had a way of talking that made women want to tell him whatever he asked. She could only imagine his powers in his youth. She had to be careful around a Di Rossi.

"Why do you talk to me in English?" she asked.

"Because I want to speak your language," he replied cryptically.

"Even though I can speak yours?"

"Americans are lazy," he said. She chuckled, thinking about his earlier comparison of Dario working like a poor American.

"It's hard for me to say what I feel," Lark admitted as she twirled her wine glass, full of ice water. Dario in his pinstripe shirt glanced across the table in her direction, a single arm draped over the empty chair next to him. He returned his eyes to the table. His father eyed them both conspicuously.

"So I've noticed," he smiled.

"It's easier to say it in another language. Then it's like I'm working. Like I'm interpreting for myself," she continued.

"You interpret so much more than just language when you speak," Signore Di Rossi continued to compliment her. Dario came by it honestly, it seemed. Lark smiled again.

"Perhaps because language is more than just language."

"It sounds so beautiful when you speak Italian."

"It sounds beautiful when anyone speaks it," she argued, amused.

"I must disagree."

"Italian is the most beautiful language there is," she admitted, taking a drink. Meanwhile, Dario simply kept his eyes on her as the two conversed.

"*Si*, but it can be butchered. Like English."

"English is best when it's butchered," Lark insisted.

"*Basta!* You surprise me, *Allodola.* There is beauty in English," his father said.

"Said no one, ever," she replied.

"Email. Cinnabon," he said in his thick accent, chewing.

Lark laughed and Dario shamelessly drank in her expression, the professional mask slipping for a moment as she kept them company.

"Everything you named were products," she said. "English is the language of commerce, business. Anyone who speaks it has been forced to. If they want to get anything in this life. It is an empirical language."

"It is merely fancy Greek," his father said with a wave of his fat, wrinkled hand.

"Or unfancy German," she laughed.

"Is this what drives you? You hate your own language?" he pointedly asked.

She shook her head. "No, I love all languages. I just like having the choice."

"*Italian is your favorite,*" he rattled off.

"*Si.*"

"What is your second favorite?"

"French."

"You crave romance," he replied, the word "crave" rolling out of his mouth so easily sent a tingle up her spine. *Holy hell, gramps,* she thought.

"*Oui,*" she giggled with her hand resting under her chin. She looked over at Dario then, her defenses lowered by his hornball father.

She studied the two of them, the resemblance suddenly very strong, suddenly more than a resemblance. They were the copies of some other man in varying stages. Some other man from long ago. They both wanted to sleep with her, which she found hilarious. She shook her head as she locked eyes with Dario who couldn't stifle his smile.

"What do you think of marriage, *Allodola*?" his father suddenly said.

Shoulda saw that one coming, Lark thought.

"*Piantala,* papa," Dario scolded him in a low rumble.

"I don't think of marriage, signore," she replied anyway with a scoff. Dario tried to remain neutral through her answer, flagging down a waiter for the check.

"No? You don't want a family someday?" his father asked, forlorn.

"*If this is going to turn into a conversation about me wasting my best years, then you can save your breath,*" Lark returned to the

Italian he requested. He let out a hearty guffaw.

"Of course not. You are brilliant and accomplished."

"That's a surprisingly modern mindset for a man like you, signore," she said.

"But eventually, you will want more. Trust an old man."

"*Italian men want a woman who will stay home, cook, make babies. Raise them. I don't cook. I can make coffee at most. I haven't stayed home since the minute I turned 18 years old. Perhaps I could grow a baby, but unless it can live on coffee, I would be useless,*" she confessed, her icy assessment made flowery by its Italian delivery. She switched to English for her diplomatic conclusion.

"I'm afraid I wouldn't do motherhood very much justice. Or marriage," she said, taking another leisurely sip of water.

"*Allodola*, if you can master seven languages you can manage a household," Signore Di Rossi gave her a sincere look as he chewed.

"Perhaps," she conceded, shrugging a shoulder and suddenly not in the mood to talk.

"I think I'm going to turn in gentlemen," she excused herself politely. "Tomorrow?" she directed at Dario.

"Tomorrow," he replied. "*Buona sera.*"

"*Buona sera*," she lightly answered with a warm smile as she left the table.

"Tomorrow? *Cosa succedera* tomorrow?" his father asked when Lark was out of earshot.

"*Niente.* A meeting."

"How can a meeting be nothing?"

"Because I will have to have the meeting to know that it is something."

"*You had a meeting behind my back today*," his father revealed in Italian. Dario sighed.

111

"You would not approve."

"I am still the one who runs this company."

"Do you want me to take over or what?"

"No more meetings without me."

"I don't want to waste your time; let me waste mine."

"Bullshit, Roberto."

"Fine. I will need you tomorrow anyway. Should this one work out."

"Di Rossi is a classic brand. Do not tangle us up with some fad of the day, Roberto."

"Yes, Papa."

"I sent you to very expensive schools, as you wanted. Do not embarrass me."

"No, Papa."

"*Allora*, did you make love to Miss Chambers yet?"

"No," Dario lied with a sigh.

"You are an idiot," he said, wiping his mouth with a napkin. "You know very well we don't need her services. She is overqualified."

"She is the best."

"She is beautiful. Everywhere. Marry her," his father said after a gulp of wine.

"She is indeed. She has a million options, and she deserves the best."

"What better choice is there than you, Roberto? This is the reason every man desires to be rich and handsome."

"I had my time. I was lucky. Besides, she doesn't want it, you heard it yourself."

"You long to discuss her. Even with me. Even though you despise me," his father leaned in with a grin.

"I do not despise you."

"You admit that you're in love with her."

"I hardly know her."

"You hardly knew Alessia. I've seen you this way before."

Hearing his dead wife's name out of his father's mouth was about all the bitter irony he could stand for the night.

"*Piantala*. I am her boss. She is too young for me, and I am far too old for her."

"*Sciochezza*, you don't know old. You are simply old for a young person."

"I am also feeling tired," Dario said, sitting upright and draping his sport coat over his arm.

"'*Uomo Italiano.*'"

"What are you on about, old man?" Dario asked as he stood.

"I asked her about marriage and she replied with the expectations of Italian men. Why would she do that?"

"That's fine detective work, papa," Dario sighed with a pat on his shoulder. "*Buona sera.*"

"Do you know where I would be right now? If I was a young man?"

"Chasing some woman who is too polite to tell you to fuck off, while your children wait with their crying mother for you to come home."

"*Roberto*—"

"I'm only teasing," Dario recovered with a kiss to his father's forehead. "Don't stay up too late."

"Bah. *I do what I want,*" his father replied over his shoulder, as his hand did a stereotypical glide across his throat.

10

Chapter 10

Dario stayed awake far too long that night, the panoramic view of the city's electric red and white grid surrounding him like a foggy, blinking fortress. He couldn't stop thinking about Lark, talking about the expectations of Italian men. Talking about "growing a child."

He remembered adoring Gino's baby phase, and nostalgia had only made that adoration grow strong. It was too easy for him to imagine Lark's swollen belly, her clay-colored breasts engorged with milk.

You're too old to keep up with a baby, he told himself, the thought making him scoff.

Gino was a handful, and that when Dario had been a young man. Running and climbing, jumping off of *everything.* But his nonna was always there, though she wouldn't always be. And there was more than enough extended family now to help out.

Besides, Gino's a boy. A girl perhaps would be different...

He sighed, hating his mind. He could barely think of anything else. He was positively weak at the thought, too weak to sleep, somehow. He didn't know what it meant. But of course, that wasn't entirely true.

No doubt she was scared, he continued to ruminate. Because she grew up an orphan. She had no mother.

She doesn't know the process. Going from an individual to part of a unit. How could she?

Maybe she would lash out, over some distant trauma come rushing back. Maybe she would panic and run away. For awhile. Then she would come home. Then they could make up. They could make love.

Home.

Dario groaned as he tossed in his bed, his muscles flexing across the broadness of his honey-kissed back as he buried his head in the pillows. The darkest hour of the night shone through the window by the glowing moon.

It didn't matter. He'd overshot his chauvinist boss routine by a mile. He thought he was doing something noble by keeping his intimate connections as meaningless as possible. He thought the women deserved payment, some form of retribution for the slight. It wasn't their fault he still loved his wife. Regular women found the exchange insulting. Whenever he was out of the country it was his custom. He felt no shame, but he could not face his son's innocent eyes if it ever got back to him. His favorite was Amsterdam. A little out of the way, but worth it.

The moment Lark caught him with another woman, her respect for him completely diminished, he felt. She called him "sir" out of obligation now. She questioned his decisions, his judgment. She couldn't feel safe with him, professionally, emotionally. Hell, probably even physically. She clearly just wanted to get paid and get out of there. And tomorrow would likely make things worse.

Numbing the pain was so much easier sometimes. If he

explained it to Lark, she would understand, he was sure. She'd practically done the same the first night they met. He'd felt both sympathy and empathy, among other emotions. They'd shared more than their bodies, they'd shared an understanding. Only... he hadn't been numbing himself with her. He had been truly alive. And all his subsequent affairs couldn't drown out the electricity that coursed through his body the first time he'd grabbed her hand and led her to the terrace, and eventually the cellar. And the burning it left behind only intensified, the closer they worked together.

He racked his brain thinking of an appropriate context for his confession. There was none. She would have to be ignorant, for now. And he, more discreet.

He turned once again on his back, the shadow of hair on his bare chest trailing down below his sheets where he was naked, his preferred way to sleep. He ran fingers through his hair as he sighed, his long lashes veiling his pea-colored eyes. They barely moved.

"Alessia," he whispered in the darkness. There was no answer besides the faint honking of city car horns.

Surrendering to insomnia, he reached for his phone and dialed.

The phone rang and rang. Finally, there was a click.

"Papa?"

"Gino."

"*Come va*? What time is it?"

"Almost four, I think."

"What are you doing up? Jet lag?"

"Perhaps. How's nonna?"

"Worried, you know nonna."

"Tell her I will be home soon."

"Take your time, papa, we're fine."

"So eager to get rid of me. You are not having house parties, are you?"

"No."

"Gino..."

"Just some friends over. A hangout."

Dario smiled a smile that was close to dissolving into tears, his emotions brimming.

"*Ti voglio tanto bene, Gino.*"

"I love you too, dad."

"No booze at this hangout of yours."

"I know."

"And no girls besides your cousins."

"Papa—"

"Fine, their friends as well. And your curfew is still midnight."

"I know, papa. Everything's fine. Enjoy your trip."

That meant he was done talking. Itching to get back to the business of easing into adulthood.

"I'll call you tomorrow."

"Please don't."

"*Buona sera.*"

"*Buongiorno*, you mean."

He hung up the phone before returning it to the nightstand.

A moment later, he picked it up, exasperated.

He opened an incognito window on his browser and typed into the search box: *New York escort service Manhattan.*

* * *

"Sparing no expense, are we?" Lark said as they settled in the back of a spacious limo that pulled up to the hotel entrance the next morning. Dario was across from her.

"My father insisted. He'll be joining us later" Dario began, donning a distinguished pair of black-rimmed eyeglasses that were testing Lark's resolve. "We're meeting Sergei's distributor. His name is Chekhov."

"You look exhausted."

"I am exhausted."

"I've got something you can take if you need it. I still don't know what day it is, but I can sleep, at least."

Dario was wordless as he stared back at her, reticent to speak. Lark became nervous.

"What's that look?"

"I'm afraid I'm going to need to you to do some spying again today."

She sighed. "What language will I be pretending to translate this time?"

"None. I need you to pretend that you don't understand anything but English."

"What?"

He had no reply, as though he knew he was asking her to do something unethical. Perhaps illegal.

"Feel free to say 'no,' Miss Chambers."

"Mr. Di Rossi... what kind of nonsense are you mixed up in?"

"None, if you do your job properly."

"It sounds like I'm not doing my job at all."

"You will pose as my assistant."

Lark made a face. "Your *American* assistant?"

"Why not?"

"What if Sergei is there?"

"He won't be."

"But what if he is? He'll recognize me from yesterday. He'll know I speak Russian."

"Then we will not go through with the charade. But there will be no need. Because he *won't* be there."

"This all just seems very silly. A man of your stature, chasing amateurs around the world for their business."

"I have no stature. I work in a factory."

"You would have me believe that you're doing all this out of ignorance?"

"*Allora*, you are an interpreter of languages, so I do not expect you to understand. But over the last seven years, I've managed to get Di Rossi Textiles the lions' share of the control over production, from harvesting to manufacturing. I've both saved and made us a ton of money, and until I have officially taken over, it is my father's job to collect the stature."

"Now, I have set my sights on the way we advertise. And I will save and make us a ton more money the same way, by taking risks and seeing opportunity where no one else sees it."

Lark adjusted herself in her seat, satisfied by his generous explanation. After a few moments, she got an idea that made her eyes roll.

"I can't believe I'm suggesting this but... perhaps it would work best if I were your... girlfriend."

He broke out into a self-satisfied grin.

"First of all, you're dressed much too boring to play my girlfriend," he mused. "Secondly, why would I be bringing my girlfriend to a meeting?"

"Because... I don't know. Because you're a wealthy Italian businessman who does what he wants. Obviously, you've only just arrived, you would have just met me, and... you're taking me out right after."

"Oh, like una prostituta," he understood.

"...Sure."

"Did you pack the gold dress?"

Her mouth gaped open.

"Che cosa ho detto?" he asked. *What did I say?*

"I do not look like a prostitute in that dress!"

"You are right. We will have to find something much more expensive."

Her mouth gaped open again and her brow furrowed.

"What?" he said cluelessly.

They stopped into the first designer store they could find on the way, and fortunately for them, they were in New York.

Lark quickly followed behind him into Dolce & Gabbana.

"Welcome to Dolce & Gabbana, sir," the older store clerk began. Dario immediately fished a platinum card from his breast pocket.

"Be ready to ring us up? We are in a hurry," he said before she could finish her spiel.

"Of course," the clerk said, eyeing the name on the card. "Mr. Di Rossi. It is an honor."

Dario made a quick lap around the store, grabbing four different looks.

"You're a celebrity," Lark said quietly, following behind.

"Only in the garment district," Dario downplayed.

"I like the red," she said over his shoulder.

"Someone call Miss Chambers a doctor," he said as he turned toward her. He held the garment up to her face and eyes. He gave her calm expression a once-over that it didn't need as she studied him back.

"If I'm playing the part, let's go with the red," she rolled her sugar brown eyes.

"A semi-sweetheart neckline in red is a bit too obvious. Even for me," he said. He held up a blue number, the color of the Caribbean, and almost picked it until something caught his eye.

He made a beeline for a tight, knee-length leopard print dress in a stretchy blend, with a jewel neckline and three-quarter sleeve. Since she had little time to re-work her austere bun, and she was useless in stilettos, he thought the bold choice would balance it out.

"Try this on," he said.

Indeed he was right. She looked like a wealthy heiress that'd begun a modeling career out of boredom. Her eyes were the color of an actual leopard's. She was stunning.

"That's the one," he said.

"What should I do with my clothes?"

"Leave them here to be burned."

"Hilarious, Dario."

When she used his first name, he didn't correct her. He was taking her shopping to become a Bond girl, so he had no room to be a stickler. And he was about to further push the boundary.

"*Allora*, I... think you should also have the blue. And the red," he suggested diplomatically.

"How much are they?"

He wasn't suggesting she buy them. Clearly, she wasn't going to let him buy them.

"$1500," he said.

"Altogether?"

"Each."

"Dario, that's a week's salary. They're very lovely, but I can't afford that."

Yep, he called it.

"Try them on, at least?" he pushed.

"There's no point," she insisted, giving him an icy stare.

He let out an exasperated sigh. He could suggest no more than that. He certainly wouldn't be able to convince her to stay in character the rest of the day. Or that escorts had wardrobe changes. At least he got one designer dress on her.

He paid at the register and Lark walked out with her new dress on, rushing behind him as they again entered the limo.

"*Va bene*," he sighed. "Ready?"

She gave him a deep breath and a shrug, looking much more like her best self in the sexy attire.

"Lights, camera, action."

* * *

"*Signore Chekhov*," Dario began.

"*Gospodin Di Rossi*. Where is your father?" asked Chekhov.

"Detained. I told him if we make a deal, tonight you could meet us at the hotel to celebrate."

"Who's this?"

"This is... Natasha."

"Just Tasha," Lark corrected for no discernible reason. Lark held her hand presumptively for Chekhov to shake it, which he did as he huffed a laugh.

The group sat at opposite ends of a wide table, Chekhov on one side while three intimidating-looking men sat behind him against the wall. Dario was glad to have Lark with him. Now everyone looked like they belonged in a gangster movie.

Dario felt Lark was still a bit too conspicuous looking. The more she blended into the background, the more she seemed like an interpreter and not like a high paid prostitute.

He summoned Lark to sit on his lap and she complied, letting the smile grow unencumbered across her lips.

He couldn't account for Lark, but he was doing absolutely no acting as he took in the sight and weight of her, felt the expensive fabric across her smooth body. Their eyes met and he gave her a wink. She let out an adorable giggle as she crossed her legs, cozying up to him.

"It seems like you are in a hurry, Signore Di Rossi," Chekhov began.

"Does it?" he answered without his eyes leaving Lark's. Chekhov smiled.

"Where is this impressive translator I keep hearing so much about?"

Lark's heart beat faster, but she didn't flinch.

"I saw no need to bring her. Sergei told me you speak English."

"Pity. I was looking forward to it. I was told she was very beautiful."

Dario brought the corners of his mouth down as he shrugged. "For an interpreter, perhaps."

"Not like this beauty here."

Dario looked at Lark again and grinned, mostly gloating about his wardrobe choice. To the men, it simply looked as though he were grinning about... other things.

"No, Tasha is one of a kind," Dario remarked. Lark furrowed her brow, gave him a 'tsk' with her tongue and a roll of her eyes, as though black attitude came with her girlfriend experience package. All the men in the room laughed, including Dario.

"*The man has thing for black women, I think*," Lark heard Chekhov say in Russian. The men behind him laughed.

"*He must want to fuck his translator but he cannot*," one of them commented in a low voice. Lark didn't flinch as she stared blankly at the exchange, looking as though she didn't understand.

Sergei must've described her.

They knew what she looked like, just not enough apparently to put Lark and "Tasha" together. She was simply relieved that the word they used for "black women" wasn't pejorative.

"How much did she cost?" Chekhov asked.

Lark felt Dario's energy change and it threatened to level the room. He stiffened where she was sitting against him.

The company behind Chekhov seemed to take his response in stride, almost like a challenge.

Shit. These people were *fucking* criminals. And she was about to die. Or worse.

She needed a diversion. She made a quick acting choice.

"I don't think you could afford me, boo," Lark said raising both eyebrows, her voice calm and full of shade as she looked in Chekhov's direction.

Chekhov looked over at Lark, who felt every inch of his disapproval. He didn't seem to get disrespected often.

Okay. 'Criminals' may not be a strong enough word, she thought.

"That's enough, *Allodola*," Dario slipped, flustered.

Luckily, no one noticed.

"I'm sayin' babe, I think he was tryin' to disrespect you, for real," Lark continued as though unaware of her surroundings.

"*Basta*," Dario replied, with a bit of force.

The men behind Chekhov began dissolving in snickers, which loosened Chekhov a bit.

"*These women, they are sexy but not worth the hassle,*" he said in Russian then finished in English, "How can you stand it?"

Dario seemed to instantly know what he was referring to.

"*Ma dai*, have you dated Russian women??" Dario ribbed him.

"Of course," Chekhov chuckled.

"*Allora*, it is very nearly the same. Except Tasha cannot drink me under the table," Dario said. The Russian men guffawed at that, while "Tasha" maintained an indignant expression.

"What?" Dario asked her innocently as she glared at him. She evaded his attempts to touch her as he tried to console the unamused "Tasha" with a stereotypical Italian flare, all while trying not to laugh.

Chekhov loosened all the way up after that.

"Listen, Mr. Di Rossi. I'm sure you have gathered that our operation is not exactly... squeaky clean," Chekhov began, his hands folded out in front of him.

"But Sergei, he is my nephew. He started out as a kid, putting fake Adidas stripes on our black market goods. He made us a fortune. But now he wants to go straight. He's a natural. A genius, really."

"What he showed me looks suspiciously like a certain Versace line from 2014," Dario confessed his suspicion.

"He has no schooling," Chekhov divulged, "everything he does he learned from watching. I told him, 'school is a waste of money. Buy fabric, study the greats.'"

"I see."

"He needs help. I told him, 'go to Italy,' but he wants to put Russia on the map for fashion. I am very proud of him."

"You should be."

"Will you help him?"

"Of course. Only... he might consider changing his brand name. For safety in the future."

"I'm way ahead of you," said Chekhov, "Perhaps you can convince him."

Dario and Lark were again wordless as they made their way back to the limo. Lark didn't even look in his direction as she inched across the smooth leather of the back seat. He sat beside her and motioned to the driver to take them back to the hotel.

Lark sat with her arms folded and her legs crossed in her designer leopard print dress, unamused and not facing him. So she didn't see the laugh lines across his eyes as he gave her his biggest smile to date.

He chuckled a bit at her distaste for being rattled. He gave her a modest round of applause.

"*Brava*, Miss Chambers," he grinned.

Finally, her neck swiveled in his direction that was holding her still unamused head. He simply stared back at her, grinning.

"Natasha?" Lark finally said, raising an eyebrow.

"I thought it was a fabulous fake name."

"Fabulous? It was painfully obvious."

"Which you changed, on the spot. Nice touch. Where did you learn to talk like that?"

"Like what, an African-American? It's the one thing I didn't have to learn."

"You don't talk like that with me," he said.

"Should I?"

"If it's who you are."

"I haven't the slightest clue who I am."

"You just... turn it on and off like that? I felt like I was in an American movie," he marveled.

"*Una dozzina di lingue e questo è ciò che ti stupisce.*" *A dozen languages and this is what amazes you,* she said under her breath as she shook her head.

She sighed, obviously exasperated with him, and what he'd just put her through. This was sooo not part of her job description. Looking at her somewhat paled expression he laughed at her again, ending with a snort.

"What on Earth is so damned funny?"

"You."

"Me? You almost got us *killed*."

"Honestly, *Allodola*, he wouldn't have killed us. Though I might have killed him," he divulged, looking into her eyes, still grinning. Lark swallowed.

"You saved me, *vero*? If you hadn't stepped in when he offered to buy you, I would have broken his neck. And then where would we be?"

Lark's wildly beating heart was no closer to recovering as he eyed her. She faced forward, letting out a big breath.

"Men," she finally answered.

"Did he say anything to contradict his story?" he asked.

"No. And clearly he was telling the truth."

"*D'Accord.*"

"So you put me through that for nothing."

"Technically this was your idea," he defended himself.

She exhaled again, smoothing wisps of stray hair from her face where beads of sweat had formed. He noticed her shaking hands before she returned them to the shelter of her crossed arms.

"You're trembling," he said, feeling shame and guilt.

"I'll be fine," she insisted.

He predicted this would happen. He was sure her confidence in him was now officially non-existent, their small window of intimacy dwindling.

Wordlessly, he wrapped his sport coat around her shoulders and put his arm on the back of the seat so that she could recline on his chest. She was in no mood to protest.

She let out another deep breath as she closed her eyes and slowly, gently, rested her body against him. She tried to let the scent of his costly cologne calm her, rather than send her into a hormonal frenzy.

She imagined that they did this sort of thing, all the time. That he was hers, and she often used him as a cushion. And that he often let her.

Suddenly the car lurched to a stop in front of the hotel and Dario's heart with it. There was no further excuse to hold her like this anymore. She felt his chin resting against the top of her head.

"Chekhov and his men will be joining us tonight for dinner. Along with Sergei," he said.

"I suppose I can stay upstairs until the coast is clear?" she suggested in a weak voice.

"Nonsense, you will celebrate with us."

"Are you sure? Chekhov will know you deceived him."

"He will understand," he grinned. "In fact, I think he will enjoy the unveiling."

Finally, Lark raised herself up with his sport coat still around her shoulders, meeting his gaze with trepidation, her toasty brown eyes a shade slightly darker than her own skin, her bold leopard print dress singing against her body.

Before he knew what he was doing he raised a hand to her face, caressing her smooth jawline.

"I was only joking earlier, you must know," he began, his low baritone humming across her insides, "I would never, ever let anything happen to you. Ever."

The trepidation in her eyes only deepened. His speech did not seem to put her at ease. She looked as though she were about to speak. For a moment her eyes were the same as they had been at his mother's house, when she asked if there was a private place they could go.

He'd been with another woman then too, the night before.

Why did it keep happening? The moment he gave in to shameful lusts was the moment right before Lark unexpectedly landed in his lap. Literally, this time. It must mean something. His thumb gently grazed her bottom lip.

"Get out, *Allodola*. Before we make love."

"You'd do that?" she asked, barely above a whisper. Her lashes came down like a veil as she glanced at his lips. Her eyes darted back to his. "Right here? Right now?"

Dio mio, she still wanted him. To the point of madness. Daring him to make a move. To fire her.

He couldn't. Not just yet. He gave himself another nanosecond, before pretending he hadn't seen what he saw.

"Have we met?" he joked.

She laughed. He smiled.

And just like that, her eyes returned to normal. The moment passed him by.

Painfully, he watched her pull the handle on the passenger door and flood the back of the car with light and cool air.

"Miss Chambers," he called out after her. She stuck her head back inside the car.

"Wear something boring tonight," he said.

"Yes, Mr. De Rossi," she smiled.

Dario blew a long slow breath out of both cheeks after Lark closed the door, leaving him in the backseat alone.

11

Chapter 11

Dario had been right, Chekhov did enjoy the unveiling. When they met at the hotel to celebrate their new business arrangement, he called for Lark to come downstairs after he and his father had properly broken the ice.

As requested, Lark came down dressed in her boring pencil skirt and crisp white blouse, her chunky black heels click-clacking toward their table. She had blow-dried her hair so that it was extra straight and thin, as it had been the night Dario first saw her.

Chekhov's eyes widened with recognition. The men around Chekhov at the table laughed and laughed. All except Dario, who only had a sly grin.

Clearly, Dario had already told him what he'd done.

"Tasha... tell me it isn't true," Chekhov pleaded dramatically.

Lark scrunched up her face, her shoulders went up in contrition as she winced.

"Please accept my deep apology for deceiving you and your men, but my boss put me up to it because he didn't know if he could trust you..." Lark continued to backpedal on and on in perfect

Russian while Sergei and his men died laughing all over again at Chekhov's expression.

Chekhov continued to stare at Lark in disbelief periodically through the night, which garnered giggles from her and from his nephew. He shook his head.

"She is beautiful, was I right?" his nephew said in English.

"She is very beautiful. *One of a kind*," he said in Russian, echoing Dario's words about her from earlier that day.

Dario looked over at Lark, trying and failing not to adore her. He had an arm behind her, his posture open as her body pointed towards his. It was their most unprofessional posture to date. But then again, she wasn't on the clock.

"She has a future as an actress, no?" Dario said. Chekhov laughed.

"Indeed! It's like night and day," he replied.

"And it was her idea."

Lark hid her face with one of her hands while Dario continued to make fun of her.

"This..." Dario said, his free hand moving up and down like a game show model as he showcased what she was wearing, "this is how Miss Chambers chooses to dress."

His father and Sergei the designer laughed the loudest as Lark smacked him in the chest.

"Criminal. I will make something for you," Sergei insisted.

"It would be an honor, thank you," Lark cordially smiled.

"My apologies, Miss Chambers, for what you may have over-heard today. If I offended you."

"No worries," Lark said.

"*Your boss is in love with you*," Chekhov said in his native tongue. "*Are you in love with him?*"

In the time it took Lark to be taken aback by the statement, take a deep breath, and then let it out, he had his answer.

"*You should marry him. You will not do better.*"

She looked over at Dario, who returned her gaze fondly. With slight apprehension in her brow, she hesitated. Then continued the stealthy conversation with Chekhov in their hearing, with all except Dario and his father understanding.

"*His wife died many years ago. He will never get married again,*" she explained back to them.

"*Before the year is over, he will ask you.*"

Lark giggled nervously, and finally, Dario could not hold back his curiosity.

"What are they saying about me?" he grinned.

Lark turned to him then, still high off of their brief interlude in the limo, close enough to him now to feel his warmth and smell his scent that lingered underneath his expensive shirt.

"*They are deeply saddened by how ugly you are,*" she answered him in Italian, her tongue quickly advancing from the back of the mouth to the front, as she went from rounded flowing Russian to the sharp, poetic jabs of Italian.

She returned his adoring gaze as the language danced on her tongue like graceful razorblades, and then she took a drink.

"*Slushay*, if he doesn't, you come find me. I will break both his legs for you," Chekhov vowed to her in English. Lark burrowed her face in Dario's chest in embarrassment.

"*Cazzo*, if I don't do what??" Dario asked, having only understood the last half of the threat. The table laughed again.

* * *

Two days later, they landed in Paris for what Dario called a "pit stop."

It wasn't on the itinerary. But he wanted to make a personal appeal to a client who'd severed long relationship ties with Di Rossi textiles. A bespoke tailor's shop that used Di Rossi's cotton and wool for suits.

Lark fell asleep on the plane and had one of those horrible dreams of hers where her mouth was full of unrecognizable gunk.

Dario was there, sitting next to her, and they seemed to be at some sort of stadium, like one for a baseball game.

She knew she was supposed to be translating, and instead of excusing herself as she obviously would have in real life, she simply sat in her stadium folding chair, her right hand pulling and pulling this gelatinous, flopping mass from her mouth that wouldn't end. It was so severe that she was gagging, in the dream at least. She had no idea if it was happening at all in the real world, though she'd soaked part of her pillow.

She hadn't had one of those dreams in a long time.

The first and only meeting that day she merely sat and watched. They couldn't seem to reach a consensus on pricing. Lark was pretty sure they were just keeping her around for decoration at this point. Or out of pity. Everyone spoke English.

They went out to a modest dinner afterward. Dario took them to a small street-food vendor, famed for his roasted chickens. They split a freshly baked baguette with butter and used their fingers like French peasants.

Lark tracked down her friend Teresa as soon as she learned they were going to be in the city. They managed to carve out a single hour to get together in the three days Lark was in town. She'd caught the ladies up to speed a few times via Skype, and Teresa had been the least surprised. Or helpful. They met at a cafe just outside Lark's hotel the following rainy afternoon.

"So? Has he crossed the line, yet?" Teresa tried to catch up on the latest.

"Not yet. In New York... almost. Which may have been my fault, I can't tell."

"Details?"

"Um, well... I can't tell you all of it, but... I don't know. Something happened that sort of shook me up a little and he was... comforting me."

"*Zut alors!* I don't understand you. I still can't believe how he looked at you that night. You are with him every day and you've already forgotten."

"*I* still can't believe how unhelpful you were that night."

"That I didn't recognize him? What, we never went to the factory. I just made the clothes, I pick the fabrics like."

Lark sighed, rubbing her forehead, reliving the beginning of this disastrous life trajectory.

"He looked familiar," she reminisced.

"No shit."

"He looks a bit like his father I suppose, but..." Teresa shrugged.

Lark mimicked her shrug with a rolling of the eyes.

"Honestly, would it have mattered? If he would've gone up to you and said, 'I'm your boss and I want you tonight,' would you have said, 'no'?"

"Probably wouldn't have fucked him at his mother's house."

"Then I know something about you that you don't," Teresa grinned before giving her cigarette another drag. "How many more days left?"

"Two."

"You know each other well now. You must sleep with him while you still can, while he is still your boss. It would be

134

intoxicating."

"Teresa, you are a slut, and also, you forget. I *did* the boss thing already. And it was horrible."

"Because you picked a troll, *Alouette*. This man is not some bureaucrat, looking to be a big shot. He *is* a big shot. He's a self-made man, from a line of self-made men. A true boss. He is Italian and beautiful. He wants you."

"He's a rich, powerful man-whore, who hires interpreters he only sort of needs, and flies them around while he bleeds money. How is that rare?"

"I cannot believe my ears. What has he done to you?"

"Nothing," she lied.

"Then you are trying not to be in love with him. Why?"

Lark sighed as she sat back in her chair, stirring her cafe au lait.

"*That's* why," Lark said with a nod of her head, drawing attention to whatever was over Teresa's shoulder.

She turned around to see Dario arm in arm with a blonde, walking hurriedly past the cafe as they fought the rainy wind with their collars upturned.

"Honestly, I think he's doing it on purpose."

"You are jealous."

"Of course, I'm jealous."

"What can the man do? He is your boss now, and he respects that. You're in such close quarters, perhaps you torture him. He wants to sleep with you and he cannot."

"Why does everyone keep saying that? Of course, he can."

"*Does* 'everyone' keep saying that?"

"Never mind. Supposedly I'm the only one that knows about his little lady habit, but he's been terribly indiscreet as long as I've known him."

"He is simply on a bender I'm sure. He will go home soon, where he is just an overworked single father."

"You're doing a very good job of defending him. You sure you don't want to sleep with him yourself?"

"If I didn't think it would come between our friendship, I would throw myself directly at him," Teresa admitted. Lark chuckled.

"I'm sure he has gathered how relationship phobic you are by now," Teresa reasoned.

"He didn't have to. I've made mention of it many times."

"Then you have no right to be angry with him," Teresa said.

"Maybe. That doesn't mean that I have to approve. Honestly, it's a little... disturbing."

Teresa laughed and shook her head at her hypocritical sentiment.

"What?"

"Do you remember the day we met?" Teresa asked. "You and Channing on the train to Siena?"

"Of course."

"Remember we saw those two gorgeous men in the gift shop on the way home?"

"'Fuckable Mario and Luigi?' How could I forget? The short one was the most beautiful, I'd never seen such a thing."

"You went straight up to them and said '*che bello.*' They followed us all the way out to where our train was waiting and ran after it until they couldn't keep up."

Lark adopted a far off goofy grin in rememberance.

"I only do that sort of stuff when you're around, did you know that?"

"You told me as much that day. It's what you love about me."

"It is. What can I say? You make me feel like a natural woman,

Teresa," Lark mused.

"Give it up, Lark. You are powerless. The moment he said 'this one.' It was over."

She thought about the first time she saw Dario see her, when they were two strangers about to forge a connection out of thin air, and then tried in vain to destroy the evidence.

Lark's face crumpled as though her dutiful facade was being pressed under the weight of her emotions and fears.

She shook her head, running a hand slowly across her smooth hair until it returned thoughtful under her chin. She sniffed. Where to start? She looked at her friend with watery, reddening eyes.

"I'm glad I inspire you to let your hair down, *Alouette.* You deserve to feel ecstasy, you deserve to have love."

"Love? *I've never seen it done. Not once,*" Lark rattled off in French.

"And yet you are afraid. And yet you know that it exists," Teresa said. "Tell him how his affairs make you feel."

"They don't make me feel anything," she lied.

"Honestly, Lark. You know a dozen languages. There is nowhere in the world you can go where you cannot communicate. You are valuable beyond measure, and there is nothing a man can do to take that away from you."

"So?"

"So, what do you have to lose? What else do you have to do that's more pressing in your miserably lonely life?"

"Teresa, that's cold. And yet... oddly motivating. As ususal."

"I have to go. I'll be late," Teresa lamented.

Lark stopped her when she attempted to summon the waiter for the check. She excused herself with a kiss on Lark's cheek, returning her leather bag to her shoulder.

"Tell him who you are. Tell him how you feel. You can afford to take the risk. You will never forgive yourself if you don't."

* * *

Dario tried to snap himself out of it as the beautiful blonde woman, known to him as "Eloise," began to undress in front of him.

Not only could he not think about sex, but he could also only picture Lark's disapproval of the whole thing. And his mind was busy thinking of defensive rebuttals to her questioning of him.

It was a hell of a thing to be distracted by while looking at a woman's bare tits.

"Ti piace?" she said in Italian. She didn't wait for him to answer. Otherwise, she would've known that he wasn't paying attention.

She got on her knees in front of him, unbuttoning his trousers, and he was beginning to doubt his ability to go through with this.

He had a problem. Lark would be leaving him soon. And he was going to miss her. He needed to drown his sorrowful dread in pussy.

But judging by his lackluster erection, moving on was going to be a bitch.

"You are too tense, *mon ami*," Eloise tactfully deduced. "Come, let me help you," she said peeling back her Chanel dress. Lark could kill in a Chanel dress, he thought.

Did he *have* to move on, his mind wandered? When he imagined trying to pursue Lark, to woo her, he saw himself successful, but only for a time. She would try to resist, and he would refuse to let her leave. But the moment she was out of his sight, she would be dressed, pressed, her hair pulled back without a strand out of place, insisting that she must be going. He saw it as plain as he saw this strange woman's red lips around his cock.

Unless he planned on perpetually flying around to exotic locations in order to retain Lark's permanent employment— which he was considering— there wasn't a single thing about her that made him think he could keep her from running as she'd promised.

She's doing a good job, Dario's cock brought the message to the forefront of his brain. His brain considered it a waste of an opportunity to let the moment go unused. It started feeding Dario images and his body responded, sending his soul on a gently rippling tide of pleasure. He liked to resurrect old images of his wife when he wanted to pity himself, but those weren't working today. He'd positively worn out every image he still had left of Lark.

Wanna bet? His brain challenged. His mind perused the catalog and landed on the two of them in the back of the limo, where he threatened to make love to her there. But instead of helping, the memory jarred him.

"*Basta*, Eloise," he said to her.

Whatever phase of his life in which this had once worked for him was clearly over.

He told himself this would be the last time. But it seemed last time was the last time.

"The night is young, signore," Eloise replied.

"It is, and I'm sorry," he insisted. "You will be compensated for your trouble."

"No need," Eloise hastily got up and commenced dressing, her jovial mood all but disappeared. She seemed more than a little annoyed. Dario sighed as he pulled up his pants.

Pull yourself together, he said to himself. If he wanted Lark, he simply needed a game plan. She couldn't run from the past forever. Eventually, she would tire.

As Eloise was seeing herself out, Dario could see from his chair overlooking the adjacent Parisian apartment buildings that Lark was standing just outside, her right hand still in the air and poised to rap on his door.

"Sorry, I'll come back later!" Lark said in a raised voice, her eyes averted.

"No need," Dario projected from his chair across the room, "she was just leaving."

Lark backed into the hallway as the beautiful French woman emerged, her bouncy blonde hair somewhat disheveled and adjusting her big feet into her heels. A string of French curses could be heard under her breath as she passed by, eyeing Lark the entire way. Lark just stared back at her as if she were possessed.

"Something you need, Miss Chambers?"

"Pardon me, signore. I tried your cell and the room phone—"

"I know. It's fine."

"It's just that Signore Di Rossi told me that you needed my..." Lark suddenly stopped, her hand still gesturing in mid air.

"Actually, there is something I need, sir. Now that you mention it."

Dario sat up in his chair.

"I need to know why you insist on your... women coming here. When there are other hotels you could..." Lark's words turned rotten in her mouth.

She sounded like a silly girl who thought the world revolved around her. And she knew it, as she spoke.

"My women?"

"*Si.*"

"*Allora,* Miss Chambers. I may have been more open than I usually would be about this... aspect of my life because you saw something that you shouldn't have, and I felt the need to clarify. You then made it a point to set parameters on our relationship, which I have agreed to. So now I must remind you that you are here to accompany us, not to approve of my personal decisions."

"Of course, signore."

Dario recognized Lark's short tone. And she hadn't moved. He sighed.

"But..." he urged her to continue.

"I simply don't understand why you insist on flaunting your... sexual exploits in front of me."

Dario cocked his head as his brow furrowed.

"It bothers you, *Allodola?*"

"Of course it bothers me! It bothers me as it would bother anyone in my position."

"So it does not bother you especially."

"No."

"Ah. *Va bene,* I will be more... careful in the future. For your sake. But I imagine since you will only be with us two more days, this will not be a problem for long. If ever again."

His words unexpectedly pierced her. Had he not ever planned to hire her again? See her again?

She, of course, could be mature and ask. But, if she had such maturity, perhaps her life would be a different one. Her dreams un-haunted.

"Honestly, you're a bit... old to be engaging in such things. It's concerning," she chose instead to say.

"Is that so," he said.

"*Si.* You're a grown man. A widower, with a son that's

141

practically an adult. What does he think of how his father—"

"My son has no idea about what I do with my personal life, and it will stay that way," he said, meeting her eyes.

"Do you think your son is an idiot?"

Dario squirmed under Lark's unexpected interrogation.

"No, I think my son knows that I am a broken man still grieving the loss of his mother and he would be correct!"

"Or you are using the memory of his mother as a crutch—"

In a flash, Dario was on his feet standing directly in front of her, threateningly.

Lark certainly didn't recognize this side of him, she distantly realized as her heart increased in speed with every inch he drew close to her.

She didn't think he would hurt her, but in case he would, she was ready. She'd faced worse than him already in her young age. His eyes blazed as they met hers but she didn't flinch.

"I do not want to hear you make mention of his mother ever again, Miss Chambers. *Capisce*?"

"*Si*, signore," Lark bit back embarrassment.

"You have *greatly* overstepped your bounds. I do not know what manner of conversations you and my father may have had, but you have not had them with me. Do not speak of my wife again."

"I apologize," Lark matched his gaze, a flicker of defiance in them.

"Do you have something else to say, Miss Chambers?"

"No, signore."

"No? You have simply lost respect for me is that it? I am no longer worth the discussion?"

"Your words. Not mine."

"What choice do I have, *Allodola*? Hm? I do not want these

women. I only want one woman. But she is... a ghost. She floated away like a dream and now I cannot have her."

"*Mi dispiace, signore,*" Lark conceded, trying to catch her breath, "I cannot imagine what it's like, the loss of a spouse."

Dario sighed, he sat back down in his chair, deflated. Lark stood stock still and didn't speak further. She stared at the floor, pretending to be awaiting further instruction.

"You interrupted *me*, Miss Chambers, what is it?"

"Oh— uh... I...." she almost said, "it doesn't matter." But she couldn't lie.

"Come back when you can remember."

"Thank you, signore."

Lark walked calmly out of the room in a fog, teary-eyed, shrinking every second she thought of how horribly the last five minutes of her life had just gone. Perhaps their Russian spy antics had indeed gone to her head. Not even at the U.N. had she behaved in such an unprofessional manner with a superior. The way she'd made a fool of herself, and insulted the memory of her boss's wife in the process.

It was a good thing there were only two days left. They didn't need her. She was pretty sure she could manage never being in the same room with Dario again for the next two days without being too obvious.

She got off on the wrong floor three times before she finally made it back to her room. She instantly locked the door, shed all her clothes and drew the hottest bath she could. There she soaked underneath the tall open window, the faint sounds of Parisian traffic many floors beneath her.

She sighed a long sigh, enveloped by steam and absent-mindedly applying a sponge to her shoulders and choking back tears. She couldn't wait for this job to be over.

A gorgeous bath in a gorgeous hotel and all she could think about was him. And his hurt feelings. What about hers? Not that there was much that still hurt her. But for some reason, the way he fiercely defended the mere utterance of his wife in conversation hurt so much that her body ached, tense from shock.

Lark had begun to create an idealized version of her. She didn't know what she looked like, but she must've been Italian and beautiful. Rich. Smiling. Never quarreling. Did they have servants?

She tried to tell herself that her "honest talk" disaster was a good thing. It was an eye-opener. None of this was real. They were in no way equals, in no way the same. Lark was of no use to a man like Dario, beyond a good lay. Being around him was like being in a dream. Being wanted by him was the same. But he was tethered to his work. If his wife was still alive today, she would likely be at home and miserable. He couldn't be free if he wanted to. It's not as though he could travel, backpack across Europe with her. If he couldn't go, it meant she would be the one to have to stop. And she couldn't conceive of doing such a thing.

Not even for love.

12

Chapter 12

Finally, they were on the tarmac at the Paris airport early Monday morning. Another overcast spring day. They would be in Italy in four hours.

Dario had gotten used to having Lark a few steps behind him, her gentle alto his international mouthpiece.

They'd found a rhythm. He grew to anticipate the chain of understanding that moved from his mouth and out of hers to his clients. She'd gone from the occassional request for him to repeat himself to none at all. She'd learned him well enough to anticipate him, his business well enough to convey his vision.

Every few seconds his brain would remind him that she was leaving. And every few seconds his heart rose and fell.

"I'm officially impressed, Miss Chambers," Dario said as they boarded.

"With what?"

"You have managed to dress yourself sufficiently for three weeks out of that picnic basket with a handle you carry with you."

Lark laughed. "It has a few new pieces now, thanks to you,"

she said, taking a plush seat next to him on the private aircraft.

Dario had gone back and purchased the two dresses he saw at Dolce & Gabanna. He delivered them to her room as part of a 'thank you' gift bag he and his father had put together. 'I couldn't help myself' the note read. A tacky sentiment no doubt made tackier by the spat they'd had in his room two nights before.

"My father insists on a farewell lunch for you when we return," Dario said.

"That sounds lovely. May I pick the restaurant?"

"I didn't ask, but I don't think so."

Lark laughed, "I'm going to miss him, I think. And you, of course."

"Of course."

"I feel I should apologize, signore."

"For what?"

"For the other evening. For overstepping my bounds."

"Never mind about that."

"I hope it won't affect what you report back to the agency."

"I would do no such thing. You're a consummate professional, Miss Chambers. Considering our... brief dalliance, beforehand. You have handled yourself well. You have nothing to fear."

"Good. Of course I'm also concerned about... our relationship."

"Relationship?"

"Yes. We've built a mutual respect over the last few weeks, I believe. One that I wouldn't want to put in jeopardy."

"Easy, Miss Chambers. You are making me blush," he teased her for her tepid speech. She smiled.

"I just mean... I remember how nervous I was when this all began. Nervous wasn't the word for it, really. And now that I've finally earned back the respect that I... threw away, I'd hate to lose it again because of foolish words."

"Do you trust me, *Allodola*?"

The question took her aback.

"I... well, my trust is unusually hard to come by, signore."

"I know. Which is why I ask."

"I suppose I do. I suppose you earned that."

"Good. Then trust what I am telling you. You never lost my respect, *Allodolah*. Ever. It has only ever grown."

"Thank you, signore."

The engine roared over their conversation and the plane lumbered down the runway as they waited to take off.

"Can I ask you something? About that night?" Lark asked.

Dario perked up, but only on the inside. "Of course."

"What made you come back? To our table."

"I wanted to meet you."

"You wanted to 'meet' me?"

"*Certo*. I never thought I would see you again if I didn't. I didn't know what would happen that night."

"Which is why you had protection?"

"Miss Chambers, if I haven't shown you by now that I always like to have a plan, then I do not know what else to say," Dario replied. Lark's shoulders shook with laughter.

Lark reached for the zipper on her bag, retreating to her headphones one last time. She hesitated before fitting them into her ears.

"I don't think I ever got a chance to say thank you. For... that weekend," she was cryptic in her description of their lovemaking.

"You did."

"I did?"

"*Si.* I remember. In fact, I have not heard you miss a single opportunity to say thank you. For anything. It is one of the things I love about you."

Lark was silent while the engines roared over their conversation. Dario stayed pre-occupied with his newspaper as he spoke, trying to distract from the strength of his affection for her. It seemed to work. The plane tipped them back into their seats as it climbed into the air. Finally, she looked at him until he was compelled to look over and their eyes met again.

"Thank you," she mouthed, in response to his compliment. He gave her a grin.

* * *

The farewell lunch was catered and took place in the courtyard at Di Rossi headquarters, the main office out of which the senior Mr. Di Rossi worked. Dario too had an office there, a bit smaller but with a beautiful lobby that contained a baby grand piano left wanting use.

The entire office was invited to lunch, though few of them had ever even met Lark. Signore Di Rossi went on and on in elaborate exaggeration about their international wheelings and dealings, though he hadn't been present for many of the meetings. When he regaled the tale about meeting the Russian mafia boss, Dario didn't bother to correct him, which made it hilarious.

After two hours, the luncheon still showed no signs of stopping. Lark fished for her phone out of her bag.

"Signora Chambers, you need to leave, no?" Signore Di Rossi asked.

"I'm afraid so."

"*Signora, e stato un grande piacere,*" he said making a grand gesture with his hands.

"Likewise, Signore Di Rossi."

"*Buon fortuna, piccolina.* Roberto, escort Miss Chambers to wherever she asks."

The two of them left the courtyard and went back inside, stopping just outside his office, in the interior hallway that led out to the busy receptionist area.

"You will be going straight to the airport?"

"Essentially. I like to get there early to beat the American tourists," she said. He smiled.

"Surely we paid you well enough to splurge on a first class ticket."

"*Molto bene,*" she complimented him, referring to his use of the word "splurge."

"It's only a few hours, signore. Once I land, I won't be so frugal," Lark continued.

"Smart," he said smiling.

"So, I guess... this is goodbye," Lark sighed.

"For now. Hopefully not forever," Dario said.

"Of course."

"I will be sending your agency a glowing recommendation."

"I appreciate that, signore."

"We will leave your brief career in espionage between us, *d'accord?*"

"Perfectly fine with me, signore," she smiled.

"Dario, please," he corrected her one last time.

"*Va bene.* It was a pleasure working with you, Dario Di Rossi," she said as she shook his hand, "I imagine I'll never have another assignment like this one."

"The pleasure was all mine, Lark Chambers."

Lark stopped in her tracks, staring, their hands still connected.

Absent-mindedly all handshaking slowed to a halt.

His eyes locked onto hers like a tractor beam. The look from that wild night, the one he now only distantly recalled, was back in her eye, full force.

"*Che cosa? Allodola?*" he furrowed his brow.

She swallowed, looking away as if fighting off a spell, wrenching her hand from his.

"Lark. Please, don't shut me out. Tell me."

Her eyelids fluttered closed, her chest noticeably heaved. She backed away a bit, frozen as if scared, eyeing some random spot in front of her, eyeing anything but him.

He looked at her intently, searching his mind, his heart beating wildly.

What the hell was happening right now?

She obviously wasn't leaving, but what was keeping her there?

When he realized what it was, what he'd done, he shuddered in anticipation.

And he also wanted to kick himself for not doing it sooner.

"Lark," he said again, slowly closing in on her frozen position against the wall in the hallway, her posture stiff as if he were some jungle predator not to disturb. He ran a solitary finger down her cheek and softly spoke, careful to sound truly curious, rather than boastful.

"Do you like hearing your name out of my mouth, *cara mia?*"

Her eyes met his again, a calm glow in them like a leftover campfire. His finger continued to blaze a trail across her skin, from her jaw, down her neck. Without warning, he put his mouth everywhere his finger had been, and she moaned, rather loudly.

The low buzz of commotion near the receptionist's desk conspicuously stopped.

Someone definitely heard that. *I can be loud, when I fuck,* she'd told him.

He couldn't *believe* this was real. How could this be *real*?

Hastily, he pulled her by the arm inside the doorway of his office and closed the door, leaning her up against it.

He turned the key that was resting in the lock. They could hear the sound of their own ragged breath in the soft quiet.

"Now it's your turn," he panted. "I want to hear you say mine."

"Dario?" she said in a breathy rasp.

He shook his head, "Not that one. The one my family calls me."

"Robert?" she said.

Now it was his turn to stop in his tracks.

Only family called him Roberto. His wife had. He'd braced his ears to hear it again. From a woman. But she had used the American pronunciation.

Absolutely no one called him Robert.

No one except Lark.

He scoffed a bit as he smiled, his heart hopelessly melted. He took hold of her face in both his big hands and kissed her, furiously, each one quenching a long-held thirst, each one demanding another.

Suddenly the Lark he'd known turned to the woman he remembered as Vanessa, biting his lip and eyeing him like a last meal.

But he hadn't wanted her, he wanted Lark.

"Not so fast," he said as she grabbed for his belt buckle.

"My flight leaves in two hours," she breathed.

"So? Miss it."

"The embassy in Qatar will be expecting me."

"You are out of your mind if you think I'm letting you leave."

"You were just about to," she said, as if to accuse him.

He kissed her again, slower this time, until her arms slinked around his neck and their tongues met. Suddenly the phone in his office warbled. He let it ring and ring. Finally, he broke free from her, breathless.

"My hotel, *conosci l'uno*?" he asked.

"*Sì.*"

"Wait for me there. I will let them know to expect you," he demanded.

"Like one of your whores?"

Dario said nothing as they stared into each other's eyes.

He slinked an arm around her middle and pushed her up against him and his hard erection, as he had at his mother's house. When he asked her, "Lo senti?" *Do you feel it?*

He hadn't quite known what "it" was, not then. It was an energy all its own. Volatile. One he was powerless to continue to maneuver.

"I will be there in an hour. And if you are not there, I will track you down," he said in a low tone.

Her chest heaved against his. "I won't be there," she whispered, defiance in her tone.

He relinquished his grasp on her and unlocked the door, kissing her again before opening it.

"We'll see."

* * *

In 45 minutes, Dario was walking up to the hotel, too anxious to do anything beyond make sure he hadn't made a mistake letting Lark out of his grasp a second time.

He went up to his room, looking around for traces of her.

When he searched the suite he found none. His heart almost sank until he heard the faint sound of water sloshing.

He opened the bathroom door and steam barrelled out, Lark's office attire hanging off the shower door.

Her hair was in a loose updo that was now frizzy and wet. Her toffee colored bare shoulders and long arms decorated the lip of the freestanding soaker tub as she looked out at the afternoon, that shone through the picture window of the penthouse suite.

"*You're early*," she said in Italian.

He sauntered over to the tub and she followed him with her eyes as he sat on the floor against the bathroom wall in front of her, unbuttoned his sleeves and hiked one leg up at the knee, the other outstretched.

He wore his black-rimmed eyeglasses, his crisp white shirt, and black suspenders, surveying what he could of her body. He'd been dreaming of it for weeks now. Finally, he met her eyes.

"I was afraid that perhaps you meant what you said."

"I did mean it. I've not been here ten minutes."

"What made you change your mind?"

She shrugged one shoulder, her vague version of an explanation. "Always been a glutton for punishment, I suppose."

"Punishment?"

"Of course. I was never supposed to lay eyes on you in the first place, certainly not again, after that night. And then you turned out to be my boss."

"And now I am no longer your boss."

"And now you are no longer my boss. I nearly made it out of the door."

"Was it really so difficult to be around me? I went out of my way to put you at ease."

"By flirting with me and fucking other women in front of me?"

153

"Were you jealous, *cara mia*?"

His answer seemed to agitate her. She leveled him with her glare.

"Cover your eyes."

"I've seen you naked once before, remember?"

"You haven't. Not entirely."

"I've not seen your belly button, it's true."

Lark silently returned his gaze as though she meant business. She must know how long he'd been waiting. And she wanted to make him wait some more.

He closed his eyes with a smirk, gently lowering his lids. Lark craned her neck to the side, looking for signs of cheating. But he seemed to be complying.

Swiftly, she was up and out of the tub, her bare flesh on display unbeknownst to him. She grabbed a towel, but only to lay it down on the slippery floor. She walked out of the bathroom bare naked and glistening. He smiled when the sound of sloshing water ceased, convinced he was in the bathroom alone.

He didn't quite recognize this iteration of Lark, he had to admit.

No, he wasn't her boss anymore. There was yet another side of her to get to know, one that he wasn't paying her to keep out of sight.

"Can I open my eyes now?" he loudly asked.

"*Si*," was her faint reply from the suite.

He found her on the edge of the bed, with her legs crossed, wrapped in a giant hotel bathrobe and ordering room service in Italian. He sat down next to her.

"You want room service to catch us in the act?" he asked.

"I'm hungry."

"Admit that you enjoy living in the lap of luxury," he said, wrapping his arms around her middle as he nuzzled her neck.

"I enjoy living in the lap of luxury," she limply replied.

He stopped mid-kiss puzzled by Lark's tepid reply. He raised up.

"Have I offended you?"

"Repeatedly."

"Is that so?"

"We've been in incredibly close quarters for the last three weeks. Did you really think your arrogant playboy routine could still work on me?" she snapped.

"It worked an hour ago."

"That was... a moment of weakness."

"Several moments, I seem to recall."

"You should've just let it be. Right there in the office, instead of trying to control it. What could they do, fire you? Now the moment is gone," she complained.

"I should have 'let it be' as you say? So you can get off, and then get on a plane?"

"Just as *you* have been doing this whole trip? You're really all just the same, aren't you?" Lark scoffed.

"Who?"

"I don't know. Men like you. Men in charge. Powerful, reckless. Looking to be worshipped. Offended that a woman could want something beyond you. Or worse, nothing at all."

It was then Lark confirmed the truth for him, that she had indeed lost respect for him as he feared.

The woman that he first met wasn't there anymore, he was imagining things.

Perhaps she was right to sleep with him then as she had done, before he'd had a chance to disappoint her. Perhaps he would have to settle for a single fond memory.

Or perhaps, he should've kept walking. He shouldn't have doubled back, stopped in the store with the glowing green sign to buy condoms. The whole business suddenly made him furious.

He relinquished his position next to her and headed for the bathroom.

"*Allora*, it seems I have misunderstood you. I certainly don't want to force you to be here if you do not want it. I'm going to take a shower. When room service gets here, eat. And then you may leave. And be quick about it. I would prefer it if you were gone before I finish."

Lark was stunned by his statement.

Leave and go where, exactly? She'd missed her flight, thanks to him.

"*Va bene*," she said instead.

Lark stared at the closed bathroom door long after he'd closed it. Then she sat at the edge of the bed, staring at her compact luggage, listening to the sound of running water.

She felt stuck between realities. She felt despair, enough of it to cry, but she didn't.

When Dario called her by her name for the first time ever it was like a lifeline, one she'd tried to resist but she couldn't. And she thought for a moment that she was saved from her pathological ability to self-sabotage, that Dario had been the one to save her. If anyone could save her from herself, it was him.

She had indeed gotten closer than she ever had before. For a moment it seemed she would conquer the she-devil within and behead that dumb cunt. But the wind of the blade going by simply blew her hair, short by only a breath.

The she-devil lived and got her kicked out of paradise. Lark stared and stared at her suitcase, too much in shock to relive the recent past and try to do it over. She was so close. So close that it seemed utterly impossible to ruin.

She didn't know what she was going to do, but it wouldn't be the first time. Luckily she'd saved up nearly every penny they'd overpaid her. When room service arrived, she quietly ate, dressed, activated the long handle on her carry-on suitcase and walked to the elevator.

When she got to the lobby floor the elevator door opened, and an attractive Italian woman with dark eyes was staring back at her. Her outfit was almost identical to Lark's and she got on the elevator while Lark could only stand there, watching motionless as she held a key card in her hand, what could only be used to gain access to the penthouse.

"*Lei scende?*" the woman politely asked as Lark stood frozen. She was obviously waiting for her to exit the elevator.

"*Certo,*" Lark snapped out of it.

She heard the sound of her own heels click-clacking in the lobby, the sound of the tiny wheels on her suitcase as her vision began to blur with tears.

* * *

Dario emerged from the bathroom with nothing but a towel around his waist once he'd heard Lark gather her things and go out the door. Not long after, he heard the penthouse elevator doors opening again.

Cazzo, she was early. They were never that early. There was no way the two women hadn't ran into each other, he thought, a ribbon of embarrassment infecting his mood.

He shook it off, grabbed two glasses from the bar and started pouring drinks. Once he turned around, he nearly dropped them when he was once again confronted with Lark's presence.

He felt a little exposed, standing in front of Lark with nothing but a towel secured around him. She'd never seen so much of him, despite their wild night nearly a month ago. If she noticed at all, she wasn't letting on. In fact, she had an energy that was more naked than his own, despite being the only one fully clothed.

Her face was raw with emotion, but her expression was blank. Her head was held high but her gaze was faced downward as if she couldn't look at him.

"Sai cosa vuol dire essere scartato?" she began.

Do you know what it's like to be discarded?

She stood there as if transfixed, a hand still holding the long handle on her diminutive suitcase.

"My caseworker didn't tell me that both my grandmother and my aunt could have taken me in, but they declined," she began in Italian. *"She didn't want to upset me. Sometimes my mother would come to me and cry, as though her world was falling apart without me. She would come to me and say, 'I'm going to get sober, I'm going to get help, and then I'm going to get you out of here.' And then time would pass. In the meantime, I would be moved. I would be the new kid at a new school. Sometimes an awful school, sometimes a prestigious one. I would spend as much time at school as I could. It was stable and consistent.*

"I would start a new language," she recalled, a tear rolling down her cheek. *"I would be moved again to another family. This one spoke Spanish in the home. Or Korean. Another Arabic. Every day I would hear their language and I learned it. Quickly. Everyone would be so impressed. I thought that they would be impressed enough to keep me from moving again. I thought my mother would be so proud of me she would have no choice but to clean herself up, and find a clean place for us to stay. To me it was a simple task, but*

I understood. Her life had been very difficult before me. And the drinking made her feel better. The boyfriends made her feel better."

Dario stood still and listened as she spoke.

"Then one day, I woke up and was 18. I had nothing, no money, no family to take me in, but I had seven languages. I was able to get into college. My mother never did anything for me, and yet somehow I owe her my life."

Finally, she met his green eyes that were warm and unflinching. She switched back to English.

"I know what it's like to be discarded. To be moved from place to place like cargo, to learn how to be so streamline, such a convenience that it would be more of a hassle to get rid of you than to keep you. And yet, I was discarded anyway, again and again. But until today, I had never known what it was like to not only be discarded but replaced. I just wanted you to know, Signore Di Rossi, that I appreciate the experience for what it is. I will carry it with me."

Dario looked at her a long while.

"That was... very moving, *Allodola.* I had some idea about your life, but nothing so dramatic as that."

Lark quickly wiped her eyes with a dainty finger, maintaining her stoic composure.

"And... I suppose this is the part where you make an equally dramatic exit to go along with your speech?"

"I beg your pardon?" she gasped.

"You didn't come back to stay. You've come back to wound me."

"And I suppose this is the part where you think I should feel guilty?" she echoed his response. "How dare you!"

"Do you think I have no wounds of my own? You want to compare, is that it?"

"There is no comparison!" Lark exclaimed, her long arms at her sides with hands in balled up fists. "None!!"

She said it as though she'd been waiting to say it for years, that it was how she felt, no matter if it was true. He didn't challenge her.

"*Va bene,*" he replied.

"You sent me away, and you had my replacement within the hour!"

"No, *Allodola.*"

"Tell me how you could do such a thing," she sobbed, tears pouring from her eyes. "Tell me."

Dario was overwhelmed with guilt. It was clearly the exact wrong thing to do to Lark Chambers. He shouldn't have called so soon but he was blind with frustration. The girl had been early. Much too early.

"I know you're rich, I know you're spoiled—"

"Of course I'm rich and spoiled. I was born rich— filthy rich, *cara.* That is no more my fault than your life is yours."

"I know you *can* do it, perhaps I even know why. But *how?* How??" Lark continued as if he hadn't spoken.

"Your *replacement,* Lark? I know nothing of your life, of what you went through, *certo.* But that also means that you know nothing of what it's like to be the product of two wealthy families, families that have been wealthy for centuries, *d'accord?*"

"No, signore."

"'*No, signore.*' Your manners are rehearsed. You mock me. You think it is no great education, the life I live. Yes, I know the novelty of wealth, and how swiftly it wears off. Pleasure at its most fleeting, I can tell you that. But I also know something, *intimately,* that you don't. That you couldn't know, or else you wouldn't talk in this way. Your ignorance tortures you, *cara.* You are a fool."

"What don't I know, Dario? For God's sake, tell me—"

"I can replace nothing. *Nothing.* And no one."

She was silent as his green eyes penetrated hers.

"I am a man with an entire ocean at my disposal. *And I am dying of thirst!*" he bellowed dramatically in Italian. "You think because you catch me, in the act of drinking seawater, that I am no longer worthy of respect—"

"I never said—"

"*Non devi!*" *You don't have to,* he said, raising his voice. "I know what it looks like. I know I have a son to raise, and a family business to save. But sometimes I miss the wetness on my tongue, the simple pleasure of swallowing and feeling content, even if just for a moment—"

"And that is the speech you choose? *You compare women to salty water! No wonder we are disposable to you!*" Lark spat, gesturing wildly.

"*You are not even listening!*" he shot back, intermittent Italian flying this way and that between them. "All you hear, everywhere you go, is your sad story!"

"*Says the gorgeous Italian widower who cannot find another wife!*"

"You threw *me* away, *cara.* Remember? You tried to ruin us before we could begin."

"Yes! And thank goodness! Turns out we're all just *seawater* compared to *il tuo amato!*"

In a flash, Dario was across the room crushing Lark in his grasp, his torso still wet from the shower and dampening her blouse, rendering it see-through. The scent of his skin, the sight of his body, and the feel of his warmth were too intense for her to properly grasp his fierce and sudden anger.

"What right do you have? To bring up the dead? Hm?" he confronted her burning eyes.

"Is she the reason you are doing this to all of us?" Lark demanded weakly.

"All of what? To whom?" he shook her with every question he asked.

"Your... bone pile. Of broken hearts."

"I've broken no hearts."

"Haven't you?"

She looked at him, intently, all but confessing her feelings in that silence.

Dario felt his confidence bloom. He was actually going to make love to her again.

"They are transactions, nothing more," he said. "I prefer it that way."

"How long do you plan on torturing the living? Because your true love is a 'ghost' as you call her? That floated away?"

"I wasn't talking about my wife."

"What?"

"In Paris. When I said that to you. Yes, I loved my wife, but she was not the woman I was speaking of. You are the woman."

"*Bugiardo!*" she spat.

"Why would I lie!"

"Because you don't care, you do what you want! Why would you parade them in front of me?"

"I don't know! Because I'm an idiot. *Because I wanted to make you jealous,*" he said.

"Jealous? Why?? *Che cazzo,* it was like knives in my *heart!*" she suddenly cried, trying to free herself from his grasp. "Vorrei che non mi avessi mai visto quella notte!" *I wish you never laid eyes on me that night!* she said in Italian.

162

Dario held her tightly by her arms at the elbows. He let her struggle and squirm and wear herself out against him as she cried, until finally she was spent, panting and sobbing.

"Please don't say that," he said almost in a whisper. "Now you are putting knives in my heart." He held her until she quieted down completely, swaying ever so slightly once their foreheads touched.

When he was confident she would keep still, he moved his hands from her arms to the sides of her face, grabbing it intently. They locked eyes, hesitating before he went in for a kiss.

"You really don't know how I feel about you? After all this?"

He engulfed her mouth in a kiss, their breath becoming frantic before they broke apart again, panting. His hands went to her waist, her backside.

"You are not like the others, cara mia. Sei il primo vero bibita che ho avuto in tanti anni. Tanti anni."

"You are the first real drink I have had in many years. Many years," he confessed in Italian as he undid the zipper on her boring pencil skirt. It fell to the floor. She stepped out of it and he sat on the bed in front of her, his bare chest facing her bare legs, his bath towel still dutifully in place.

He gulped when he saw her black lace underwear peeking behind the curtain of her white dress shirt, wet from his body against hers. His pleading eyes looked into her face as a tear dripped off her reddening nose. She raked her hands through his cold wet hair, looking down at him.

"Non posso... essere la tua acqua, signore." *I cannot... be your 'water,' sir,* she sniffled.

His hands were delicate across her hips.

"Perchè no?" *Why not,* he whispered. He leaned his head against her middle.

"Perché lo voglio," *Because... I want that,"* she winced as his mouth seared her belly button with moist hot kisses, "più di ogni altra cosa. Troppo." *More than anything. Too much,"* she breathed.

He raised from his sitting position and stood in front of her.

"Hai paura che annegherò?" *You are afraid I will drown?* he asked, slowly removing his towel to reveal the whole of his tanned body.

She stood mesmerized, gawking at his broad, naked shoulders, of all things. She wanted to lick them. He finished undressing her, unbuttoning her blouse and revealing her matching lace bra.

"No, signore. Ho paura che tu berrai e ti sazi." *I'm afraid that you will drink and have your fill,* she replied, her eyes and nose red and raw.

He didn't dare tell her that's precisely what he intended to do. She wouldn't understand. She seemed to view herself as a commodity in the eyes of others, of other men. But he knew different. And he could be the one to show her different.

He peeled her last remaining undergarments from her body, until they were both as naked as the day they were born. He lifted her off her feet and carried her the short distance to the head of the bed, gently laying her down. He loomed over her, nuzzling her nose, her jawline, and finally her long neck. She let out a long pleading moan that made him shudder.

"Let me drink you in now, *cara mia,*" he breathed, "Let me taste you on my tongue."

Tears had fallen from her eyes, into her ears and dried there.

"Just for tonight..." Lark tried to resist in a whisper.

"One night? You would let a thirsting man die?" he guilted her, in typical Italian male fashion. She couldn't help but laugh.

"Tonight and tomorrow," she insisted.

"Tonight, and tomorrow, and the next day. And all the days," he demanded with a flurry of kisses along her face.

Lark closed her eyes, disbelieving her ears. She felt herself diving off a cliff.

"*Va bene*," was all she said before he met her lips.

13

Chapter 13

When Dario put his legs between hers, his large hand gently cupping her inner thigh, the moment was so sweet she nearly died right there.

Her body completely open to his, all talking ceased. No language could compete with the feel of his body against hers once again, this time naked, this time feeling the brunt of his weight as he entered her gently, easily.

He felt much more invasive in this position, and she welcomed every inch of him. Her mouth was agape but no sound would come out. He took his time filling her up to the hilt with his length, trying to convey love but also betraying his need that felt so desperate it only rendered her further speechless. She felt another warm batch of tears across her temples and she was sure she'd never cried so much in her life.

Dario filled the silence with his own eager moanings while Lark's eyes melted closed. Her body was racked with sensation and she finally took in a desperate gasp of air, unaware that she hadn't been breathing.

He thrust her over and over until she couldn't deny that he

was telling her the truth. She was the woman.

Her body relaxed. She stretched her legs at the center, trying to accept as much of him as she could. Eagerly he took her, raising her arms along the pillows above her head and adjusting his position as she hooked her leg across his buttocks.

This time, he was the one that needed to fuck. She was starting to wonder if he'd even had sex with any of those women, he seemed so starved. She supposed it was possible that he hadn't. He fucked as though he'd been waiting a hundred years to have her again.

Soon his mouth was open as if to engulf her once he found a rhythm that he couldn't resist any longer. His brow furrowed, he began groaning, the eve of orgasm drawing closer.

She didn't want to miss a second of it. She wanted to witness every moment of pleasure she was giving him. She studied his morphing expression, from the man she knew as her boss to that of her lover, the expression of a man no longer in control. Damn, Teresa was right. It was damned hot.

Suddenly she could feel a tingling sensation that wouldn't go away and was getting stronger.

It was an orgasm that she hadn't earned, that she hadn't fought for. It would barely be the size of a kiddie wave pool but she welcomed it, focusing on the pleasure of her boss as the feeling waxed and waned with every inconsistent thrust.

"Lark," his gentle come voice called to her. Pleasure wrapped around her like a perfume cloud until it disappeared. She wanted it again.

"Dario," she said in a whisper. It was just the motivation he wanted.

"Oh, Lark..." was the last thing he said before his pace went to double time for as long as he could manage. He was trying to make her come. He was succeeding.

She was so close to the edge already that she made no effort, she simply focused on his pace and his breath until the wave rose higher and higher and was fully grown by the time she felt it up her spine. Her eyes swam round and round, her brow furrowed, and her gentle moans of gratitude became forceful cries of relentless pleasure. Her pelvis jutted out towards his and he couldn't hold on any longer.

His body convulsed and pinned itself to hers as pleasure had its way with him. He hunched over her and gave her a few long, dramatic thrusts as he held her, before the pleasure finally died down and let him go.

For a long moment, they didn't speak. They simply kissed and caressed and looked at each other as their panting breath returned to normal. Dario rolled over on his back. Lark snuggled up against him.

"Let's go again," she whispered.

"You read my mind," he whispered back.

Words between them were few as they spent the evening getting re-aquainted and making up for lost time, even learning a few new things about each other. They made love until evening, until Lark didn't care that she ached. The next morning Lark woke up in bed alone. Just as she'd done their first night together, only this time, there was a note:

"I'll be back by noon to pick you up. Wear the blue dress."

Lark got up, showered, blow-dried her hair until it was shiny and smooth, and obsessed over wearing it up or down, or parting it on this side or the other. She decided to wear it in a high ponytail, her long bangs swooped to one side.

Could you try any harder? she chided herself. It was true she was starting to think of her appearance in terms of what she perceived would make Dario the happiest. In the flirty blue blazer dress well above the knee, with the deep v-neck and long flared sleeve, she didn't know if she wanted to go full vixen or keep her hairdo demure to balance it out. But she was always demure. Why was she determined to bore him to death?

She began fashioning her ponytail into some kind of bun, to make her train of thought not seem so obvious. But when she heard Dario entering the room, she quickly pulled it all down, combing a part into her medium length hair with her hand.

She wanted to call out to him, but hesitated, not knowing how to refer to him. Dario, sir, "baby"— none of them seemed right.

She didn't want to make it seem like she was making an entrance, so she stayed put, looking in the bathroom mirror until he came around the corner and peeked through the doorway.

If his face was any indication, she'd made the right choice.

She could see him soaking up the sight of her with his eyes as he slowly made his way towards her, looking at her intensely. He grabbed her forcefully by the hips and pulled her close to him, making her squeal with laughter. She linked her arms around his neck grinning as he nuzzled her.

"Where are we going?" she asked.

"I think I want to stay in now."

"*Sciochezza*, take me out, Dario," she insisted like a spoiled mistress. He grinned.

"Call me Roberto."

"You said only family calls you that," she smiled.

Dario stared at her, leaving it at that for the moment.

"*Va bene. Andiamo.*"

"Where are we going?" she asked again.

"A surprise."

"What kind of a surprise?"

He gave her an amused look as grabbed her hand and they headed out of the hotel and into the lobby. Lark noticed they were garnering looks this way and that. A few of the hotel personnel greeted them as they exited.

"You're quite the VIP, I see."

"*Certo*. Let's just say I have thrown them a lot of business over the years."

"*Figlio di puttana*," Lark rolled her eyes.

"Italian swear words were a part of your schooling as well?"

"It was immersive."

"Ah," he chuckled.

There was a red sports convertible out front with the top down, the tan leather interior exposed. It looked like a BMW, but with an emblem she didn't recognize— a trident on the front.

"What kind of car is this?"

"A Maserati."

"For some reason I never pictured you owning a car."

"I own many cars."

"*Certo*," she said as he opened the passenger side door for her. "You seem so down to Earth," she said as if complimenting him.

"I'm not," he replied as he got in on the driver side.

"So, now can you tell me where we're going?"

"We are taking a road trip."

"To where? Naples?"

"Wrong direction."

"Hm... Rome?"

"Guess again."

"Bologna?"

"Very good."

"And Venice?"

"...We'll see."

"It's only two hours."

"Have you ever been?"

"No."

"*Allodola*, what kind of American visits Italy without going to Venice?"

"The kind that doesn't want to get stuck in a city made of boat transport with wasted white girls."

"White girls?"

"American girls."

"White girls love to drink where their parents cannot see them," he replied. His casual observation made Lark laugh out loud, which of course made him smile.

In twenty minutes they were out of the city and following a winding road that cut through gorgeous vineyards and country-side. Lark's attention was glued to the landscape while Dario drove with a hand on Lark's leg that was behaving, for now.

"I may have made a mistake, requesting the blue dress," he said. Lark re-crossed her legs flirtatiously. She seemed much more comfortable in her bold, expensive wardrobe. She wore it like a second skin.

"Have you ever made love in a vineyard?"

"No, but I suppose you have?" she ribbed him.

"*Certo*," he replied. She giggled.

"So, shall we address the elephant in the room?"

"What elephant?"

"About these other women..."

"Ah. That elephant," he smiled hearing Lark's concerns for the first time. "Ask me whatever you like," he said as he kept his eyes firmly on the road.

"Did you have... regulars? Or were they all different?"

"I never call escorts unless I'm out of the country."

"I see. No wonder you were so... busy the last three weeks."

"The night that we first met I had just ended a relationship. Angelica. Or rather, an arrangement. We'd been sleeping together for some time. She was a married woman. I could count on her discretion and she mine. She was a flight attendant. From Barcelona. An Olympian in her youth. A swimmer. I told her we had to end it."

"Why?"

"She was getting attached. So was I."

"And your solution was to break up?"

"Like I said, she was married. It wasn't true love. Merely... dysfunction."

"How did she take it?"

"Better than I expected."

"Your father and I talked about you the evening before we left for Milan, did he tell you?"

"He did."

"The way he described you, I started to fear that perhaps I had been the first person you were with since your wife."

"Five years ago you would have been."

"Five *years*, Dario?"

"*Si*. I mourned very hard. I had no interest in love. I was working even more then. The finances were a tangled mess. Gino was becoming a teenager. Sex was the last thing on my mind."

"And then?"

"And then I met Mona. She was a client of ours. A widow. Her marriage was not so happy. But still, she had a hard time living life without her husband. We... bonded. She was very passionate. Like you."

"So what happened?"

"Nothing. She ended it."

"Why?"

"Her own personal reasons."

"Were you in love with her?"

"I could have been."

"And thus began your sexual rebirth."

"*Si*. Many widows. For much the same reason as escorts. Especially if we were both still in love with who we lost. We just wanted connection. The relationships never lasted."

"Surely some of them must've fallen in love."

"Perhaps. But they also knew that nothing would come of it. Death is the ultimate rejection. No one wishes to experience it again. Nor do I want to be the source of it."

"And so you graduated to escorts."

"Indeed."

"You've done a good job of keeping your private life private."

"Until you, that is."

"What do you mean?"

"You have a way of... popping up. At the strangest times."

"I 'popped up'?" she smiled.

"*Si*. More than once."

"I am not a widow. Or an escort."

"No, *Allodola*, you are none of those things."

"So what's changed?"

"Nothing's changed. I worked, I lived my life. And then... one day I found you."

Lark smiled. "And I you."

They got to Bologna and walked the streets a bit, sampling meats and wine, and made out in one of the alleys that tunneled through the hillside town. Lark convinced him to go further to Venice, where they again made out whenever they passed underneath bridges. They stayed the evening and rode boats under the stars.

* * *

Lark stayed at the hotel during the afternoons. She was either waiting for Dario to come over after work, sometimes in the middle of work. After two weeks he proposed that she stay at his house.

"This penthouse is costing me a fortune," he said as they lay in bed. She stiffened.

"Shall I pitch in?" she suggested, he giggled. "The agency offered me another job. In Berlin. Only two weeks. I could get out of your hair for awhile."

"You are not in my hair."

"I would get another apartment," she began, "but I would have to sign a lease and—"

"Nonsense, you will stay at my house."

"Dario..."

She'd begun calling him Dario in her American accent which melted his insides well enough. But he had been unsuccessful in getting her to refer to him again as Robert, though he requested it endlessly.

"What now?"

"You know 'what now.' Your son is there. You can't keep me hidden away and then suddenly bring me home."

"*Va bene*, we will have a party."

"*Che due palle!*"

"What did I say now!"

"*You want to introduce me as the woman you're fucking?*" she exclaimed in Italian as she sprung up out of his arms in bed. "*Your mother remembers me as the whore from her party, I cannot bear the thought of facing your father again!*" she went on dramatically, complete with hand gestures.

He was horribly amused. She was becoming more and more Italian every day.

"*Ridiculo.* My father will be nothing but thrilled, and so will my family— as soon as they pick up their jaws from the floor."

"This is all too much, Dario. Bring me to your house? For what? All we do is fuck."

"*Cara mia*, stop wounding me. You know how I feel about you. But we are in limbo. And as much as I have enjoyed it, we have to be realistic."

She sat up in bed with her knees hiked up under her chin, wearing his discarded dress shirt, thinking. She looked over at him.

"You want me to be your *fidanzata*?"

"You already are that. I want you to move in with me."

"Dario, I like limbo."

"So I've noticed. But you cannot stay here either. Come and live with me. You have to at least try it. You may find that you do not want to leave."

"It's too good to be true," she said. And it wasn't a compliment. He rested his big hand on one of her delicate feet, the undertones of their skin dueling.

"Hardly," he said looking into her eyes. "In fact, I would ask you what I want to ask you, but you seem so skittish. Like you are waiting for the shoe to drop. Isn't that the saying?"

"More or less."

"Why does English have this saying? Do Americans go around throwing their shoes in the air?"

"Yes," she replied, rolling her eyes. She knew he was trying to put her at ease with corny second language humor.

"If I ask you, you will run away. Like you are doing now."

She sighed without contradicting him.

"A dinner then, perhaps," she conceded, "but not a party."

"What is the difference?" he smiled.

Dario took Lark to his house. The grand entrance was three stories of stairs decorated with the greenest topiary on each side. The balconies were made of carved fat pillars of old stone. And it looked like a large museum.

Dario introduced Lark to his son Gino, who looked like a scrawnier version of Dario, except his eyes were large and dark, presumably like his mother's.

"Gino, you are staring," Dario said.

"She is beautiful."

"She is standing right here and can hear you. Tell her yourself."

"You are beautiful."

"Thank you, Gino."

"Are you to be my new stepmother?"

"No," she smirked.

"We'll see," Dario lovingly corrected her. "But she will be staying here. With us."

"For how long?"

"For now," he answered cryptically when Lark only looked at him.

When they went to his room to settle in, Lark looked around in awe. His room had tall ceilings, frescoes on the walls and an intimidating bookcase complete with scaffolding. Elegant, but devoid of any feminine traces. Clearly, it was a room that he did not share.

"I think Gino might have a crush on you," he grinned.

Lark gave him a giggle.

"You don't find that to be... awkward?"

"According to you, he would not have to worry."

"And if you had your way? You would make him suffer?"

"He would not suffer long. After graduation, he cannot wait to leave us. Besides, I believe he has a girlfriend he has not yet told us about."

"I think he and I may be closer in age than you and I."

Dario thought for a moment.

"You are precisely in the middle of us. He will be 18 this year."

"One day he will take over Di Rossi Textiles?"

"*Si*."

"Would you ever consider hiring an outsider?"

"Perhaps, if everyone in my immediate family died. Otherwise it would probably kill them."

"So that's still non-negotiable I see."

"Every Di Rossi runs things differently. Some better than others. Whatever strengths they have tend to outweigh the weaknesses, even if the weaknesses are indeed very weak."

"The world changes with each passing generation, Dario. Who's to say business will even run the same by the time Gino comes of age?"

"So far so good. Things are much more competitive than they were 100 years ago, *certo*. Which is why I fight to adapt the company for our preservation. Then I will hand it to Gino. If Gino decides to sell, I will not object, but he will try his hand at running it."

"What does he want to study?"

"Fashion Design."

"Convenient."

"He wants to be competent."

"He wants to please you."

"What's wrong with that?"

Lark simply rolled her eyes.

"Nothing, I suppose. Running a textile company is perhaps the best way to find out whether or not you're cut out for it."

"Indeed. Come, I want to show you something."

Dario led Lark through the cavernous rooms of the house until they made it outside across a beautiful courtyard to another smaller cottage on the property, one that was more her style of living space.

Lark was stunned when he led her through the door and she found a modest, bustling design studio, complete with a large work table, mannequins, fabrics, and works in progress hanging on racks.

"Is this Gino's?"

"No," he scoffed, "it's mine."

"Yours?" she marveled, "since when are you a designer?"

"I have several degrees, one of them in design. You did not know this?"

"I confess, I didn't do nearly enough homework on you before I started work, Signorino Di Rossi."

"Sit," he said. He searched around for measuring tape then he changed his mind, making her stand. Meticulously he took her measurements. He laughed quietly to himself.

"What?"

"I made something. For you. And I think it will fit."

"For me? When was this?"

"The day after we met."

"You must've been... inspired," she said provocatively.

"I was."

He revealed a simple provencial-looking dress on the dress

form, with blue and white stripes and big blue buttons, the stripes changing directions in a tiered pattern along the skirt.

"It's very 'Dorothy from the Wizard of Oz.'"

"But modern."

"Indeed," she smiled.

"Do you like it?"

"It's beautiful."

"I want you to wear it tonight," he commanded. Her nipples tightened against her blouse. She couldn't turn down a request from Dario. She took her time unbuttoning her shirt.

"Shall I try it on first?"

"*Certo.*"

"How long until your family arrives?"

"Long enough to make love, if that's what you're thinking," he replied, watching her remove her bra. He feasted his eyes on her dainty cleavage.

"You were thinking it too, admit it," she smiled. He returned it.

"I am always thinking it," he whispered.

14

Chapter 14

L ark spent the evening falling in love with Dario.

Dario's kitchen was vast. A mix of stainless modernity and neutral stone-colored, old-world wealth, containing several islands and lit with long pendants hanging from the endlessly high ceiling.

There was another side to him when he was among family. She knew that he cooked, but he appeared to be the culinary wunderkind of the family. Even while he was dressed impeccably in a blue pinstripe dress shirt and navy slacks, the sleeves rolled high and his brow furrowed in concentration over the raw meats, vegetables, and the steaming contents of pots.

He minded all ages of nieces and nephews, from infant to young adulthood. He smiled. He laughed. Lark sat in the kitchen nook's corner seat, trying to be invisible so that she could watch him undisturbed. But that was impossible since he was stealing glances at her just as often.

"*Where's nonna?*" a random nephew asked in Italian while stealing a meatball.

"*Running late,*" Dario rattled off while adding herbs to his sauce.

"In English, we have a guest," his nephew corrected as he gestured to Lark.

"*Her Italian is better than yours, Ernesto, get out of my kitchen!*" Dario scolded him as he scarfed down another meatball.

The sense of family was palpable. There wasn't a branch missing on the De Rossi family tree. Other than the feeling that she got when she watched the same thing on TV or in movies, the sensation was completely foreign to her, except for the part where she was on the outside looking in.

Whenever she was sent to a new home, she tried to make herself a model foster kid. One of her foster mothers, Roxy, used to make her clean the whole house and even watch her children. She was very young and had been a foster kid herself. Lark never saw a single dime of the allowance every household was allotted, so she had to assume Roxy was running off with that. Lark didn't once complain, however. But when Roxy had her re-assigned, Lark felt a betrayal she couldn't describe. The confidence she had in the value system she'd set up for herself was irreparably shaken.

Still, she kept trying to earn her way into someone's family. Well into adulthood and she still couldn't imagine *not* trying to earn her place into any family. She would spend a lifetime trying to earn her way into this one.

Just then, she caught his eye. He was dropping freshly made pasta into a boiling pot. He looked at her with a look of contentment she had never seen and it stopped her heart.

She doubted her ability to ever get used to any of it, but she couldn't stop the familiar tinge of hope from driving her mind into pictures of the future. Her breath became fractured with panic. She needed some air.

Lark walked out onto the vast terrace overlooking the estate, where the evening air was warm and breezy. She looked out to the impossibly beautiful grounds as the sun took its time setting.

She nursed her wine glass as she turned to observe Dario who was still in her line of sight from the open back doors. She watched Dario handling meat, holding his hands up like a surgeon as he chased ingredients down around the grand marble island.

"He is beautiful, no?" An older woman sharply dressed in black slowly took her place beside her on the terrace. She seemed to already know who Lark was, but Lark herself was in the dark.

"He is," Lark agreed.

"He would make any woman a fine husband," the woman cordially asserted.

"*Certo.*"

"But not every woman would make him a fine wife."

Ah. Lark knew where this was going. And who the woman must be.

"That is true," Lark took no offense to the jab she knew was aimed directly at her. It seemed to catch the woman off guard. She asked a more direct question.

"Tell me, besides your beauty, what do you have to offer him?"

"Very little," Lark didn't hesitate.

"You are not good enough for Roberto and you know this. You exude it," the woman continued her tirade. She seemed so adamant to scare Lark off that she was completely willing to skip introductions.

"You must be his mother," Lark deduced anyway.

"I am. What gave it away?"

"Signore Di Rossi told me a bit about you. You fit the description. Dario hasn't mentioned you all that much," Lark replied with a tinge of shade.

"Ah. And how is Luca these days?" Dario's mother asked.

"Unburdened," was Lark's answer, getting shadier by the second.

"Spent an evening with him as well, did you?" his mother answered, she too being a card-carrying shade member.

"You are very much like your son. He also likes verbal sparring."

"Is this a sensible way to start a relationship with me?"

"I have no intentions of talking to you beyond tonight," Lark answered truthfully. "I spent my life trying to win my mother's love. And she was a loving person. The last thing I would want is to have you in that role."

Signora Bennetto gave her an icy stare brimming with class and condescension.

"You look very poised in the expensive dress my son bought for you, but you have the manners of a street urchin. No one in this city would dare talk to me the way you have."

"It wouldn't surprise me to discover that you have insulted enough people in this city to know that for a fact, Signora Bennetto," Lark maintained her professional air.

"It must be blissful to be as ignorant as you are of your surroundings, Signorina Chambers."

"I must admit, it is," Lark chuckled, enjoying herself just a little too much. "One minute I'm interpreting for the senior executive of Di Rossi Textiles, the next I'm sitting in his kitchen, insulting his mother and drinking wine in the dress that he *made* for me."

"*Li mortacci tua!*" she exclaimed as she laughed. "It is the American in you, I presume. You must think all wealth comes from hard work and bright ideas. You must find us deplorable."

"Not at all, Signora."

"Come now, let's not pretend this began with your job. You disgraced yourself when you fucked Roberto in his mother's own home."

Lark went rigid. She went silent as she had no rebuttal, at least not one that wouldn't require a complete return to her roots.

"This dress, he made it?" his mother asked.

"*Si.*"

She gave a little chuckle and shook her head.

"You must think me too intrusive, but I never would've known if he had not told me."

"I don't believe that."

"You don't have to. As long as you promise not to marry my son, I see no reason for us to not have a pleasant evening."

Lark searched herself, looking for a reason to tell this woman to fuck off, that she was out of pocket and wrong. But there was none.

When Lark tried to imagine herself in this family, it was almost painful. Smiling, going along with their every expectation, drowning in children, in excess, in dinner parties. She'd likely be asked to give up her job and she would comply, out of perceived obligation. She would be trapped. She would eventually hate him for it. His loving gaze would repulse her.

"I promise," Lark replied stoically.

"*Va bene.* I'm pleased that we understand each other, *Allodola,*" Signora Bennetto smiled.

"Don't ever call me that," Lark smiled back.

* * *

"I noticed my mother cornered you tonight," Dario brought up as Lark emerged from the bathroom. She got into his large bed next to him as he read by the light of his end table lamp. "I am hoping it went as well as it looked."

"...It did not," replied Lark, without looking up.

"*Merda,*" he said, removing his reading glasses.

"Or perhaps it did, depending on how you look at it. I believe we understand each other fully."

"What did she say to you?"

Lark merely shrugged, keeping the details of their frank dialogue vague.

"Nothing I haven't heard from some old overbearing relative before, no offense," she said, turning down the covers on her side of the bed, "*I eat women like your mother for breakfast,*" she said in Italian with an exaggerated gesture.

She looked over and noticed that Dario hadn't moved. He was staring at her.

"What did she say?"

Lark sighed. She couldn't lie. She tried to find the most diplomatic way of paraphrasing their conversation.

"She made me promise that I would not agree to marry you."

"I see," he slowly blinked with a faint grin. "And did you?"

"Yes," she confessed.

"Why?"

"Your mother sees right through me, I'm afraid. I'm not good enough for you. She just wants to protect you, Dario."

He grabbed her open hand and kissed her palm as he gazed deep in her eyes.

"*Sei il mio cuore.* She cannot protect me from my own heart."

Oh. This must be what Signor De Rossi meant. *If he tries to woo you, you will be powerless.*

"Did you tell her about the cellar?"

185

"I did."

"Why?"

"I merely confirmed what she already knew. Everyone saw the two of us retreat and never return."

"Everyone?"

"Remember what I said about family being 'inescapable'?"

"How did they find out that we worked together?"

"I never told them that your true identity was concealed that night. They assumed our relationship has always been a mix of business and pleasure. They simply did not expect that I would fall in love with you."

Lark didn't avert her gaze as he used the "L" word for the first time, an arbitrary distinction. She already knew as much. But she concealed her inner shame, as the word simply rolled off of her soul, unpenetrated by it.

"You wouldn't say that if you knew what I said back to your mother," she replied, her eyes glowing brown with hidden mischief. His grin widened.

"If you stood up to Violetta Di Rossi Benetto, then I *must* marry you," he said, grinning. He watched her squirm at his declaration.

"I'm afraid I was a bit... aggressive. In my own defense," she admitted sheepishly.

"Do not say another word until my father is also present," he said. She laughed.

* * *

The one disadvantage to having Lark at his house was that he couldn't take breaks in the middle of the day to meet her at his hotel, make love to her and grab a bite before heading back to work as he had so many times in the weeks before.

But that was the only disadvantage.

He loved waking up to her and loved going home to her. She helped Gino with his French. His mother stayed conspicuously absent, which was a reprieve he didn't know he needed. They ate dinner, they made love, she refreshed her craft each day, brushing up on her catalog of languages.

After several weeks of this, he'd all but forgotten to guard himself against the lull. Lark seemed happy. So when he arrived home one day only to find every simple trace of her completely vanished, he was dumbstruck.

"Gino, *dove Allodola*?"

"*Non lo so*, I thought she was with you?"

He searched everywhere on his property but she was gone. She and her tiny little suitcase with the long handle.

He didn't want to seem as possessive or as hurt as he felt. Her phone rang and rang, or sometimes went straight to voice mail.

Should he start to panic? Had something really happened to her? He couldn't miss work to send out a search party. Besides, there was no need. He called the LIST agency under false pretenses, requesting her for another job, but she was already booked in London.

She wasn't kidnapped. She was avoiding him. After a few days, he called his father at headquarters, in case he had any information.

"*Si*, Miss Chambers came here to find you."

"When?"

"Last week. She is flying to her homeland, I believe."

"Why would she not come to the factory?"

"*Non lo so*. She was afraid you would talk her out of it, I think. She says she is going home and to tell you goodbye."

187

He felt a punch to his gut but he recovered.

"Did you say anything to her?"

"I told her we will all miss her."

"*Bastardo!*"

"*Che cosa!*"

"She is an orphan, and you send her away!"

"*Ma dai*, shall I ask her to let me *leccare la sua figa* before I go to the grave?"

"Papa, *e abbastanza!*"

"*A fanabla*, what excuse do you have for letting her get away?"

"...None," he sighed.

"If I were in your shoes I would have already had my honeymoon. You have a light in your eyes for the first time since you were young. Marry the girl."

"I am. I was," he sighed.

"'Was'? Why have you not asked her?"

"I did not want to scare her away."

"*Va bene, bravo,* Roberto. *Allora*, go get her, before some other man makes love to her on sight."

"Who told you about that?"

"Told me about what?"

"Never mind."

"You disgrace all Di Rossi men letting a woman like that get away. She left because she thinks you are insane," he said, giving him the Italian gesture for complete and utter dementia over the phone.

"No, papa. She left because I was afraid to tell her how much I wanted her to stay. And she left anyway. But you are half right. I should have asked her to marry me. The result would have been the same."

"So now what will you do?"

"Nothing."

"Nothing?"

"She will come back to me. As she did the first time."

"Roberto, you don't make sense."

"The first time we met was not that day in the factory. We met before. And I let her get away then too."

* * *

Lark arrived in London in a few hours, trying to ignore the growing turmoil with each mile she put between herself and Dario.

As bad as it felt that bittersweet night of the dinner— the words of Dario's mother staining the evening like a pile of shit— the attempt to return to her pre-Di Rossi life so far felt the worst.

What the hell was she doing here? As long as she kept her bags packed, she couldn't be disappointed.

She didn't want to call him, because she didn't want to hear his persuasive words. Or perhaps, his angry words, for the way she left. Or worst of all... his apathetic ones.

She should at least let him know that she was okay. In case he was worrying. But what if he tried to come after her? What if he didn't?

The night she arrived, she and Channing went to a pub. Lark changed into the leopard print dress he'd bought her, which she regretted almost instantly. She spent the night paranoid she would see Dario while out in the dress. In *his* dress. It broke her heart to even imagine it. What was she doing?

"Don't worry girl," Channing picked up on her mood, "going to a bar cannot, in any way, be considered cheating."

Lark hadn't yet disclosed that she wasn't planning on going

back.

"I know, I'm just..."

"It's all over your face, girl. I get it."

"Get what."

"My partner in crime is retired."

Lark gave her a smirk, but couldn't think of the words to say.

"It's just as well. I think this is my last year here."

"Nooo, Chan. I just got here!"

"I know! You took too long. Anyway, London is just cold, and crowded... and you can't get a decent plate of biscuits and gravy. I mean, it's just like New York. I love being here, but I wanna go home more. You know?"

Lark's mood worsened. Home. It's all anyone ever talked about. Home was wherever her friends were. The people that weren't paid to take care of her. She didn't miss America, because it wasn't home to her. Only in the way that it was a place to run away from.

"I just managed to get close to you guys and you're leaving me already."

"I didn't say 'today,' you silly. My *gosh*."

"You can make biscuits at home, Chan Chan."

"Says the girl who doesn't cook. I take it you're extending your work Visa? Or you think you can get this guy to marry you?"

Lark winced.

"Not thinking that far ahead, I'm afraid."

"Why the hell not?"

"You and Teresa," Lark shook her head, thinking about their tag team advice.

"You promised, that if you ever ran into him again—"

"That I would consider marrying him, I know. I was joking," Lark admitted as the waiter brought them another round of drinks. "You should see what the two of you look like suggesting marriage," Lark scoffed. "Teresa was in a damn polyamorous relationship."

"It's just 'cause he's filthy rich and we want to plan very expensive vacations to Lake Como every year, *duh*."

"Of course! How did I not see that," Lark laughed.

"Besides, this isn't about Teresa, this is about you."

"Yeah, well I can't do traditional marriage either, let alone *Italian* tradition," Lark twirled the stem of her Grey Goose and cranberry. "If you met his mother, you would've felt like you were in the Godfather."

"If he's attracted to you at all, it's because he doesn't want that either."

"I don't know what he wants. We never talk about the future."

"Isn't that what you say you want?"

"Yes. It's just... with him, it's different. I want to know when it's over. I want to know how much time we have left."

"Sounds like you're in love."

"You're right," she sighed. "And you know what? I simply can't stomach it. It's glorious, but it's so hard. I've gone so long without any kind of love... too long. And now it's just... making me crazy."

"Like a car that's never had an oil change?"

Lark laughed at the memory.

"Your dad is a car salesman," Lark chuckled.

"Not a mechanic, we've been over this," Channing took a sip of her drink.

"How did you not know that your car needs oil changes?" Lark shook her head.

"You're not a car. You're a human. And humans adapt."

"I was just so scared, all the time," Lark sighed. "I couldn't enjoy the moments."

"It's like that for everybody."

"Bullshit."

"Lark, I hate to break it you, but you don't have some huge missing piece that other people don't. And even if you did, it doesn't matter because no one does it exactly right. You're going to fuck up a lot, actually."

"It doesn't matter now. The agency said he'd called and asked for me again, so he likely knows where I am. I ignored his calls, and now they've stopped. So it looks like I've fucked up already."

Channing knew that Lark was in some strange place of denial. She saw the way "Bob" had devoured her with his eyes that night, all Italian and whatnot. These men don't just give up. Especially the rich ones.

But she knew Lark well enough now to treat her like the animal shelter kitten she was. Put out a bowl of milk and let her be.

"Then there's only one thing left to do, which is *get* fucked up," Channing concluded.

"I'm halfway there," Lark admitted.

"To fuck-ups," Channing toasted.

The two raised their glasses before taking a drink.

* * *

After several weeks of waiting, Dario began to lose hope. He drowned himself in work, both at the factory and at home. He spent every available moment of free time working in his studio. He could've done without the heartache, but at least he was inspired again.

"Dario. Eat. You must," Signora Benetto said. His son Gino was away at his college orientation, but Dario's mother was still coming to his house every week. She had been particularly helicopter-esque since Lark's sudden disappearance.

"I'm full," he answered.

"Nonsense. You push the food around your plate."

"*Va bene,* stay if you like," he ignored her. "I'll be in my studio."

Violetta felt a deep dread in the pit of her stomach. Dario didn't eat or sleep. He was unbearably distant, even after these many weeks. Her son was in love with the young woman.

Her years of reprieve were over. There was another woman in his life. Her words came vomiting out as he turned towards the stairs.

"Roberto, you mustn't be so sad. She left you without warning. So impulsive. Foolish. You do not deserve such a woman!"

"'Sad,' mama?"

"*Certo*, you think a mother doesn't know when her *bambino* is sad?"

"You presume to know the source of it?" Dario turned to confront her.

"...There is only one thing it could be," she pretended to deduce.

"Is it your guilty conscience that tells you this?"

"What guilty conscience?" she feigned further ignorance.

"What did you say to her?" asked Dario pointedly.

His mother just stared, a deer in headlights.

"The night of the party. I saw the two of you speaking."

"Nothing!" she lied. "We talked about you. About her intentions toward you."

"And?"

"And... she said she did not intend to marry you."

Dario's jaw clenched as he turned to go back downstairs.

"Roberto, wait—"

"You are a snob, mama."

"*Che cosa ho detto?*"

"You know what you said. You made her promise not to. You threatened her. She told me."

"I did no such thing! I was worried she would break your heart and I was right!"

"Mama—"

"She has no mother Dario! *Madonna*, how can she ever be one if she has never seen it?"

"What do you know of her mother?"

"She told me she spent her life trying to win her mother's love and she did not want me in the role."

Dario was as stunned as he was amused.

Dario continued his descent down the dining room stairs, when he doubled back.

"Allora, when she comes back, you will apologize. And when she becomes your daughter, you will love her with everything you have. Or else we will move to the States. *Capsice?*"

"Why *her*, Dario?"

"Mama this would be your question no matter who I chose."

"But why this one? The American?"

"Why do you hate her?"

"Look what she is doing to us!"

"*Va bene*, which woman would you prefer? What will you do when Gino marries?"

"*God forbid!*" She said in Italian.

"Mama, I know how hard it was to have my father as a husband. And I know Mario has not been much better. But you cannot take this out on Lark. You know what it is like to be accused of breaking up a family, mama. Why would you do the same to someone else?"

Violetta began crying.

"Il mio piccolino!" *My little boy*, she said. "You used to pick me weeds from the garden. Not flowers only weeds, because you thought they were the most beautiful and interesting. Only the best for your mama, no matter who said 'you must pick the flowers.'"

"Mama, this story..."

"You are the only one I have left in the world who loves me!"

"I'm getting married, mama, not dying."

"Why should she be loved? By you? Hm? She is beautiful. Smart. Some other man will want her."

"I am not marrying her out of charity, mama. You sound ridiculous."

"She sleeps with men she just met! And insults their mothers!"

"Is that what this is about? You are angry that I will marry someone I actually like? Someone I select and not the Di Rossis? Or the Bertellos or the Bennettos, and that she will be happy? When she has done all the wrong things?"

"We do not marry our *whores*, Roberto!"

"*Basta,*" he said in response, waving his hand as though she were a fly. "She makes me happy and I will marry her, which will make me happier. And if you love her, I will be almost too happy to live. Would you like to see that?"

Bastard. She couldn't deny that she would.

"*Si.*"

Dario slowly made his way over to his mother, once a singular beauty, married off to a powerful family. Her elegance still faint underneath her slightly hunched frame. He towered over her as he gave her a kiss on the head and an embrace.

"*Va bene.* You are wealthy beyond measure," he began, swaying and hugging. "I will not talk you out of your own feelings. But Lark will be my wife. And when you are with her, you will be an adult. *Capisce?*"

Violetta sniffed, melting under the light of her oldest son's love.

"For you, Roberto. I will. I promise."

15

Chapter 15

I t was a sweltering day in New York, despite the fact that it was September.

Lark was staying with Yumi, the wife of the grocery store owner down the block from her childhood home. Yumi sold the store for a tidy sum after her husband died. Now she lived in a lovely apartment in Koreatown on Long Island. She didn't speak English very often, or very well.

Lark was in the living room staring at a blinking cursor on her laptop. She was trying to write an e-mail. Trying and failing.

She was in-between jobs, attempting to go into work for herself. She wondered if more flexibility would give her the freedom she craved. She began to contact previous clients and tactfully find out how willing they would be to have her as an exclusive client.

"*My sister asked about you again,*" Yumi projected from the kitchen to Lark.

"*You should move your sister and her family here, Emo,*" Lark responded in her near-native Korean.

"*It's no use. My sister loves Korea. Her children are there. My children are here."*

"Then you should visit."

"It's not so easy when you are old like me."

"Send her my regards."

"I did."

There was one client on the list that she'd yet to contact. And that was the one she was trying to e-mail: Dario Di Rossi.

Fashion week was coming up, and she would bet money that he would be in town. Soon she would have the opportunity to face her fear. She wanted to see him. More than anything. But all correspondence had dried up.

She thought about him every day. Where he was, what he was doing.

You're being ridiculous, she scolded herself as she looked at her blank email. Not only did she need to reach out to him, but he also deserved an explanation. Every day that went by it only got worse.

She decided to simply copy and paste the form emails that she'd already sent out to her other clients. She inserted his name at the top and sent it quickly before she could change her mind.

It was distant and potentially passive aggressive. But it counted. She'd drawn first blood.

Minutes later there was a reply in bold in her inbox. Her heart flooded her body with adrenaline.

A brief reply from Dario.

"I will be in your neck of the woods for fashion week. Sergei will be showing on Thursday. He would love to see you. He has a surprise for you," it read.

Thursday.

Sergei would love to see her? What about him?

She hit reply, staring at the blank screen, the blinking cursor.

She got up from her place on the couch, exhausted from second-guessing herself.

She would send a reply. Soon. But not now.

* * *

Dario flew to New York in high spirits.

As Lark had done ever since he'd known her, she popped up again, out of the blue. Right when he was about to give up. Right when he was going to give in and scour the planet to find her, shake her and bring her back home.

He had received Lark's tepid email the week before. He could barely send a reply for the shake in his hands. He had to wait another tortuous day to read her answer:

"I'm pleased to hear from you and would love to see Sergei as well. Unfortunately, I don't know if my schedule will permit on such short notice. I'll do my best, but please send Sergei my regards in either case."

She wasn't making it easy, but she was reaching for him. Like a child afraid to identify her captor.

There was a chance that Lark could play this game forever, though she didn't seem like the type. But what if he was wrong? What if she never tired of running?

He could at least console himself with her butterscotch skin and shining eyes. They could reunite for one evening. He could speak tenderly to her about the turmoil she had put his soul and body through these last few months.

The show was an hour away when Dario walked past the white tents filled with Press and into the venue, where the runway had been built. The show was being held in an old stately building, that had once been a post office apparently, but you could hardly tell. He went backstage where Sergei was wringing his hands, checking the look of his garments on the models, occasionally making them switch accessories.

"Thank you for coming, signore."

"I wouldn't miss it."

"Did you tell Miss Chambers?"

"I did."

"Is she coming?"

"She wasn't able to commit. But she said she would do her best to be here."

"That's good. It's better for me to not know either way. She may be offended."

"Nonsense. She will be flattered. *In bocca al lupo.*"

"What does this mean?"

"It means good luck, more or less."

"I will be lucky to make it through this show without dying."

Dario laughed. "That is essentially how the saying goes."

Dario returned to the arena where the chairs on either side of the runway were starting to fill up. Most everyone else was in clusters, chatting either to each other or to media, standing in front of cameramen and backlit with large portable contraptions.

Suddenly he saw her.

There she was, standing behind a random staff member in black wearing large earphones and holding a clipboard. She wore a stylish trench over a plain dress shirt, skinny jeans, and red flats. Her hair was pulled back in her signature style, the front had gone from long strands to sharp bangs that accentuated her glowing cheekbones when she smiled. A guest pass hung around her neck. She'd spotted him first, because she was looking straight at him.

"Lark," he greeted her with kisses on both cheeks. She stood staring, looking petrified. A thousand words were backing up trying to work their way up and out of her.

"Whatever you have to say can wait."

"I owe you an explanation."

"You do not. You wanted to keep things casual for this very reason. You musn't torture yourself."

Dario could see his absolution made her emotional.

"No crying today. The show will begin soon," he said, wiping a tear with his thumb.

"Where do I sit?"

"With me."

"Where's my surprise?"

"You'll see. Once the show begins."

Sergei was the second to present that night. He spoke with the help of the interpreter that was with him the day they had their first meeting, not a block away from where they were now.

"I must thank Dario Di Rossi, chief operator of Di Rossi Textiles, for not only providing my fabrics but also mentoring me, and teaching me about color and silhouettes, and putting together a collection. He gives a whole new meaning to the term client services."

Lark looked over at Dario who'd just gotten Di Rossi Textiles a priceless ringing endorsement in front of the entire elite of the fashion industry. His expression was that of complete lack of surprise. He glanced over at Lark and simply gave her an effortless wink, as though he knew what she was thinking.

"My inspiration for this collection is a particular woman. She is professional, smart. She wants to be beautiful, wants to be stylish. But she wants to be taken seriously, she wants to be respected by both women and men. And this is her collection."

Dario looked over at Lark who simply applauded with everyone else, completely oblivious to Sergei's description of her. The lights dimmed and the show began.

The first model came down the runway in a dress shirt and pencil skirt and Lark's exact hairdo. Dario couldn't stifle his grin when he glanced at her again and she was still oblivious. Mixed in were pieces that incorporated iconic pieces of Russia's heritage and history, including a provocative mock Adidas outfit, reminiscent of Sergei's humble beginnings.

The models came down the runway in pieces that gradually increased in intensity, culminating with a dramatic mustard yellow dress on the darkest woman Lark had ever seen in person. Sergei got a standing ovation when his show was over, and the room was abuzz about the young burgeoning designer from Russia who was self-taught and essentially discovered by the head of Di Rossi textiles.

Everyone wanted an interview with the handsome young visionary poised to take over for Luca Di Rossi. Lark stood in the shadows as mic after mic was shoved in his face and he described his vision for the company, his mission statement going out to the world. And all without paying a penny.

When it became clear that the hype around Dario wasn't going away anytime soon, Lark let the crowd around her engulf him, until she was practically pushed out of the venue. She looked on as she drifted further and further away from him like a piece of driftwood in an ocean of bodies. She would likely have to wait hours now to find resolution. She saved him the trouble and quietly made her way past the press, beyond the barricade and back out to the Manhattan streets.

She kept her arms folded and her eyes on her feet, the surreal feeling of self-sabotage confronting her again. But all was not lost. Perhaps he would be in touch, she thought, perhaps not. Her heart beat against her breast like a prisoner as she continued to walk in the opposite direction of him. Her mind began the same string of excuses, its version of an apology. *If he wants you, he knows where to find you,* the familiar mantra droned on. But she knew now the revolving door of her fearful justifications.

She moved past anonymous New Yorkers on the sidewalk, fighting the flow of foot traffic that seemed to all be going in Dario's direction. The panic was nearly unbearable. She was undeniably in over her head in regard to her emotions, which fueled both her heart and her rebellious feet.

Suddenly she felt someone abruptly grab her arm. She spun around in time to meet Dario's eyes as he pulled her close to his chest. The unseasonably warm night air gently blew his hair. Without hesitation, her arms went around his neck and they kissed.

They kissed until they were swaying in the middle of the massive sidewalk, until people clapped, whistled, and finally complained when they had to walk around them.

They broke apart and he held her hand and led her lazily, wordlessly down the street.

"You didn't have to come after me."

"I've let you run from me, twice now. I cannot bear a third."

They kissed again and she gripped his arm with her other hand as they walked. She marveled within herself, feeling the last two months blow away like a fog. It was as though they'd never been apart. Ever. They found themselves in front of Riverside Park.

"You told him about the gold dress," Lark finally broke the silence.

"I didn't. But I picked out the fabric," he confessed.

"I'm sorry," she finally said.

"For what?"

"For what?? For everything. For the way I left. For running first. Instead of just telling you how I felt. I wanted to run, but I didn't want to end it."

"...I understand."

"You don't," she shook her head, the sun beginning to set as they looked out at the scenic waterfront.

"You lied to me," he said.

"About what?"

"When I asked you on the plane back from Paris if you trusted me. You do not."

"I didn't lie. I just... I trust that you believe that you mean what you say. I'm afraid it doesn't go beyond that."

"Why didn't you want to end it?" he asked, a tinge of hope rising in him at her words.

"*Because I love you,*" she replied in Italian.

It was all he needed to hear, all there was to know.

"In English," he insisted.

"Why?"

"Because it is harder for you."

Lark swallowed. He was right. She could've said it in the other ten languages and more. But the moment she said it in her native tongue, she was sure he would turn and walk away. Laugh. Become a pillar of sand.

The emotion came so violently she was shaking. Her skin reddened as the tears built up in the creases of her tightly shut eyes. She took a moment just to cry, maybe in shame, maybe remorse. Grief. For herself, for the others, the ones she met in the same place or worse.

Finally, she confronted her fear, letting Dario be the one to disappear. Though she didn't dare open her eyes.

"I love you," she said in a low voice.

When there was no answer, she didn't panic. Her breath slowed. She let herself believe he was gone. So she could stop struggling. So she could move on.

Her eyes came slowly open. Dario was a tall blurry figure standing still in front of her. He retrieved a handkerchief from his breastpocket and she took it.

"I love you," she said again before applying it to her face, the irrational fear she had of rejection slowly dampening.

Dario remained quiet. Lark took a breath. That was one problem down. Now to deal with the others.

"But we're from two different worlds."

"*Si.*"

"You don't fit in mine, and I don't fit in yours."

"You fit beautifully in my world."

"I was only pretending. It was excruciating."

"*Va bene.* I will come to you. Where should we live?"

"I wasn't talking about our countries."

"How else are we worlds apart, *cara mia*?"

"Your... family," she began, almost as though the word was enough to make her sick.

"I don't know all that my mother said to you, but we had a talk and I assure you. It won't happen again."

"Your mother was the only one there to tell me the truth."

"What truth was that?"

"That I am not good enough for you."

"I am growing weary of this nonsense idea," he said.

"Okay... I am not... whole enough then. I don't know how to be fueled by anything except my next assignment, or where I'm going to live. Honing my skills to survive. Living in your big house, it feels like nothing is ahead of me. Absolutely nothing. Except more of the same. Maybe I don't want what I say I want. Maybe I have grown too accustomed to being a temporary tolerance."

"You could never be a temporary tolerance to me. I love you, *cara*. I love everything about you."

But then, she imagined the hate. When the look of contentment would lose its charm. It gave her a cold shiver.

No, she thought, a lump forming in her throat. She must never go through that.

"Whatever you love about me will fade away. Love just means that it will take longer. Much longer. I don't have the patience to wait."

Lark took a breath and then switched to Italian.

"You are telling me to ask for acceptance from the most unlikely place. We have absolutely nothing in common. Nothing."

"When I told you about my family, do you remember what you said the night we met? When I walked you home?" he asked.

"I said... it sounded like a dream."

Dario sighed. "This is my fault. Perhaps I made you think that it matters what my family thinks about you. Of course, I want them to like you, to love you, but ultimately this does not matter."

"I know. Still. Daughter, wife, *mother.* These roles. Being thrust upon me. I will ruin them all."

"You are thinking too much about it. Shall I tell you what family is, since you have sworn ignorance of it?"

She wiped away a tear as she nodded.

"Family is merely a choice. Sometimes it is a wise choice, sometimes not. But it begins all the same. It must be born, just like a baby. In fact, a baby is the very embodiment of a family.

You feel like an alien, but you are part of a family. You carry two people with you always. Perhaps you do not know them, but if you were to meet them, your sense of belonging would likely astound you, but yet at the same time, it would not. And if you were to meet the two that they carry, the same would happen, and so on and so on."

Lark let the breeze blow her tears sideways across her cheeks, looking across the water as she listened.

"You are right, I cannot give you the feeling that you seek, the one that I know very well. Too well. I ache for you to have it, not because I think it would make you a whole person, but because it would make you happy to understand how... arbitrary it is."

Dario hooked a finger underneath her chin, forcing her to look up at him which she did, unabashedly, her face raw with emotion.

"It does not matter how much family I have, if that family is to continue, I have to make a choice. Just as you must make a choice. Ho trovato qualcuno. Ci siamo scelti, ma lei è morta." *I found someone. We chose each other, but she died,*" he said. "She died, but I thank God every day that we made a family, because I have a piece of her to look at always, even when it hurts."

His gentle words cleared her foggy rationale. She closed her eyes, trying to hold on to the simplicity he was so patiently trying to impart. It was the most thoughtful thing any man had ever done, welcoming her back into the fold of human relationships. *You can do this, I know you can*, he chanted through his touch, through his calmly beating heart against her head. She was starting to believe it.

"I cannot conceive of how badly the family that bore you has let you down. But I would bet much of my fortune that your mother and father, wherever they are, do not let a day go by without thinking where you are and what you are doing. And that they are not concerned about your many languages, though it is impressive."

Lark cried as he continued to probe her fears. If she couldn't resist him before, it was utterly impossible now.

"Be my family, *Allodola*. The way that you already are. You have entered my life, and you can no longer leave it. I will not try and persuade you to have a child with me, *cara*. But I think that if you do, you will understand better what I am saying to you. You are a good person, Lark. Motherhood will not depress you, as you fear. But this will not be an assignment, this will be forever. And no one will make the decision for you. You will choose. And then, if you want it, you will have family. Always. I promise."

"You promise?" she wept.

"Yes, *cuore mio*. It will be very unfamiliar at first, but you have said yourself. You adapt."

"I do say that," she sniffed after a moment.

"Yes. I listen."

"You do," she laughed. She felt her inner saboteur frantically trying to come to the surface. It was still there but growing faint in her ear, its directives sounding less and less coherent.

"Then... I choose... you," she breathed.

"*D'Accord?*"

"*Si.*"

Dario put his hand in hers, the same way he had when he first grabbed her hand the night they were strangers. It felt the same, as though he had chosen her then.

"I understand you've left the agency."

"Yeah, I've been...contemplating going into business for myself. I've been contacting my previous jobs to see if they would follow me if I started my own business."

"Everyone except me."

"I...was going to call. Obviously. Eventually."

"*Va bene*," he adjusted his voice and posture to that of the professional she once worked for. "I have a business proposition for you then."

"Go on..."

"I suspect that tonight will raise the profile of the Di Rossi company for a short time. And in that time, I plan to take advantage, traveling to as many places as I can. And..."

"And, you'll need an interpreter."

"*Si*. Do you know of anyone? That can work on such short notice?"

"I do."

"Someone qualified?"

"*Si.*"

"Who is also beautiful?"

Lark huffed. "How do you do that?" she smiled.

"Do what?"

"Plan so far ahead. And get everything you want."

"I cannot take credit for this one, I'm afraid."

"How did you know I was going to contact you?"

"I didn't."

Lark gave him the Italian gesture for insanity.

"You're crazy."

"Since I've been with you, I can't stop doing crazy things."

Lark laughed again.

Epilogue

"Allodolaaaaaah!" Dario's mother Violetta bellowed from the living room.

"What is it, nonna?"

"Has Matteo eaten?"

"Of course," Lark answered, trying and failing not to sound exasperated.

"*Va bene*, I didn't know. You look... very busy."

Lark rolled her eyes. Signora Violetta Di Rossi Benetto was full of jabs, it seemed. But Lark was convinced it was loving. Compulsively so. Whatever animosity arose between the two women was instantly deferred once Matteo came into the world.

"Matteo is fine."

"Where is Gino?"

"Gino is getting him ready for his nap and then we're going. We're already late for the airport."

"Oh, why would Roberto tell you to fly in your condition?"

"I'm only four months along Violetta, it's fine."

"Still. You work like a peasant woman."

Lark was the owner of Lark Di Rossi Linguistics, the company she started four years ago. Currently her husband was her primary client.

"Yes, but I like it, nonna."

"I know you do. Just keep your feet up, Allodola you know how you swell!"

"I know," Lark absent-mindedly answered.

Just then Gino came whizzing past the doorway. A long moment later, two year old Matteo toddled past the same doorway laughing deliriously, much more than the situation warranted. It wrenched a smile from Lark's lips.

He was stout with chubby hands and feet, and all brown— brown eyes, brown skin, brown silky curls— delightfully ambiguous and adorable. He was mostly toothless, beaming and not watching where he was going at all.

"I guess nap time isn't happening," Lark sighed.

"Gino be careful in the house with Matteo!"

"He's fine nonna," Gino insisted.

A second later there was a loud crash. Everyone waited with bated breath, everyone except Violetta who rushed out of the room to the direction of his cries.

Lark touched her thumb and forefinger to the bridge of her nose. That woman was incapable of letting Matteo cry it out, which Lark was desperate to successfully do one day. She'd had many talks with Violetta about space, which seemed to have no effect. That Gino turned out well-adusted at all was a miracle.

She looked up to see Gino in the doorway smirking at her exasperation. They locked eyes and Lark let out a knowing sigh. Gino snickered.

"*Pronto?*" Gino asked.

"I don't know. Let's go anyway, before we never get out of here."

"*Allodola*, you are rich now. Make them wait," Gino suggested.

"Does your father hear you talk like that?"

"Allodolaah! I think Matteo hurt his head, I don't think he should lay down. I will make him some pasta!"

Lark turned to look at Dario's son, now 22 years old.

"Get me outta here, Gino."

"*Andiamo*, Signora Di Rossi."

* * *

Dario was already in France for Paris fashion week. A gaggle of clientele would be showing today, including Sergei and Park Tae-Hwan, who would be debuting his SALVA brand in Europe. He could go down to the venue himself, but he decided he would wait. He felt much more comfortable having his interpreter by his side.

There was no better excuse to be joined at the hip with Lark than work. She'd become a bit of a celebrity herself, the beautiful young American "translator" that'd captured the fashion mogul's heart and become Italian royalty. A "Cinderella Story" everyone called it. She outdazzled every man's wife whever they went, and he secretly lived for it.

Her African-American heritage raised her profile in America as well, and Dario's along with it. They had more business than they knew what to do with. It was a good thing Gino was coming along this time. He would be graduating early, and Dario was more and more eager to have him learn while the company was in the midst of growing pains. It would be grueling, but it would be an education like no other. And Gino was starting to show signs of his father's ambition.

An hour later he received a text from Lark.

"*Just landed. Meet me at my hotel for negotiations.*"

Dario smirked. It was going to be that kind of trip, was it?

Dario adored Lark's pregnant and horny phase. It made him want to go for a fourth. But it would be another year at least before he could openly suggest such a thing without risking his well-being.

He sat at the cafe just outside the hotel, waiting for Lark at the usual spot. She showed up in a tan dress, delightfully round and wearing her hair in a low ponytail that now hung in the middle of her back. The pre-natal vitamins made her hair grow like vines. Her boobs were like melons and he was already licking his lips, formulating a plan. They'd been apart for several days. She shed her sunglasses once she entered the cafe and their eyes followed each other. Dario stood and greeted her with a kiss on both cheeks, while simultaneously giving her a firm handshake. They sat across from each other in their respective power positions.

"What can I do for you, Signora Chambers?"

She stifled a grin. *Every time*, she thought.

"It's Signora Di Rossi now."

"Of course."

"Allora, I've gone over the numbers and, in light of increased demand—"

"LDL agreed to my terms."

"This was before Germany was added to the itinerary."

"You're welcome to bow out of Germany if you do not wish to go, Signora Di Rossi. I'm sure we could make do."

"It would be an honor to join you in Germany, Signore Di Rossi, I just wish to be paid."

"Would an extra two thousand be sufficient?"

"It would not."

"For 24 hours?"

"Only twenty, actually."

"Signora, are you able to justify these inflated figures?"

"Germany will take time away from my family, namely my son."

Dario raised an eyebrow.

"It is my understanding that time away from your son was the *incentive* for Germany."

"Be that as it may... it's still difficult."

Dario shifted in his chair, suddenly feeling as though he was being played.

"*Va bene*, Signora Di Rossi. An additional twenty-five hundred will have to be my final offer."

Lark twirled her massive wedding ring around with her thumb.

"It seems we're unable to reach a consensus," Lark sighed.

"Perhaps we could move negotiations upstairs?"

Lark planted her tongue firmly in her cheek, concealing a smile.

"...Do the numbers make sense up there?"

Dario maintained a stoic expression.

"They do. In my experience."

* * *

The Di Rossis lay in bed in silence after their lovemaking, Dario on his stomach with his eyes closed and Lark on her back, staring up at the ceiling. They had one hour before they needed to be at the venue, luckily only a few blocks away.

"Do you remember the first time we were here?" Lark broke the silence.

"Of course."

"It was the first time you ever got angry with me."

"I wasn't angry, I was... lovesick," he replied after a moment.

"I cried and cried in my bathtub the whole night after that."

"You never told me that, *carina*."

"I did. I tried to avoid you the rest of the trip. I didn't even want to be alone with you again."

"I am glad you failed, *dolcezza*."

"Me too."

Lark took his hand and placed it on her lower side. The two waited for signs of movement.

"He was *just* moving around," Lark whined.

"He?"

"Pretty sure it's a boy."

"Do you remember when you said being with me makes you feel as though nothing is ahead of you?"

"When we were in Paris?"

"No. In New York. At fashion week."

"I said that?"

"Yes."

"No, I didn't."

"You said living with me in 'my big house' was boring. The same day every day with nothing ahead of you."

"I don't remember that. At all."

Dario smiled and let out a chuckle. He was expecting her to have many more trying emotional times once they married, but luckily Lark's former reality simply faded further and further away like a dream. He felt he could appropriately take credit for it. Just when he was about to remove his hand the baby moved.

"There it is!"

"We should get going. Our public awaits," he said. "Did you remember the dress?"

"Of course."

Dario had made Lark a nude colored silk chiffon dress that was covered in sequins and as comfortable as it was elegant. When the paparazzi pressed her for the designer she said, "It's a Di Rossi original," a teasing confirmation to the fashion line

Dario was planning to debut next year. The couple took to their premier seats in the front row of the fashion show venue, Gino also in attendance by their side as two of Di Rossi's premiere clients showed their collections. Lark's phone buzzed and buzzed during the show, but the number was unrecognizable. Unless it was an emergency from home, Lark was not returning calls this evening.

After the show, the couple and Gino made the rounds, Lark interpreting for her husband wherever warranted, rubbing shoulders and elbows and doing business as always. The evening wore on and the Di Rossis made late dinner plans with some Parisian fashion elite while Lark checked in at home, and also checked her voice messages, of which there were three.

"Gino, *dove Allodola?*"

"On the terrace."

"Something wrong?"

"*Non lo so.* I think she's just checking on Matteo."

Dario made his way through the crowd to where Lark was pacing on the terrace, one finger pressed into her free ear so she could better hear. Her brow was furrowed. His heart skipped a beat.

"Matteo?" he quickly asked. Lark just shook her head.

"Okay... is it possible she could meet me halfway?" Lark said to whoever was on the phone. Dario couldn't conceive of what the context could be.

"I understand. I can be there in 24 hours. Thank you."

Dario braced himself for whatever was happening. Unless she was going to say she was dying of heart failure, he was pretty sure he could endure it.

"That was child protective services. In America."

"Child services?"

"My sister. She's in custody. She's been reported as a runaway for months, but no one can find my mother or her husband."

"I see. How old is she now?"

"Fourteen, this August."

"*Va bene.* You must go to her."

"You know what that means, *amore mio.*"

"I do. Bring her here."

"Are you sure? She's been on her own, and I don't know what kind of life she's had, but if it's anything like mine was, she will be difficult."

"*Allodola*, is there another choice?"

"No."

"Then we waste time discussing it. Go to her."

"Matteo..."

"He will be fine. I will cut Germany short and go home tomorrow."

Lark raised a hand to her forehead, her eyes doing a roll of exhaustion.

"You can do this. You were born to do this."

"Thank you, Robert."

He held her arms and gave her a kiss on the forehead.

"We chose each other, no? Now go, *Allodola*. Go get our family."

Haven't Joined the Mailing List Yet?

If you like what you've read, I would like to keep in touch with you!

- Find out about new releases, limited time deals and bonus content!
- Get access to fan exclusives from the *Billionaire's Club* series!
- Get to know me and what I'm up to, and even work with me as part of my Advance Team!

Simply click on the link, and enter your email address to sign up:

https://www.subscribepage.com/CLDMLLanding

Mama Needs a Review!

Did you like the book? Which part was your favorite? Was the sex too much? Not enough? Anything stand out to you that you've never read before, or haven't seen in awhile? Anything you could've done without, perhaps? Well I wanna know!!

When it comes to choosing the next great read, reviews can make or break, whether you're an indie author like me, or one of the big fish in a New York Publisher's pond.

Believe it or not, you can help. A LOT.

And all it will cost you is about a dozen words or more.

If you enjoyed this book at all, and think others should too, please take five minutes to leave this book a review on the page of your respective ebook retailer. Thank you!

About the Author

C.L. Donley is a future New York Times and USA Today Best-selling Author of multicultural and interracial romance. Armed with a B.A. in English and M.A. in Writing, she is new to the romance game, having written her first novel, Amara's Calling, after discovering the romance genre in September 2017. Her writing style is sophisticated yet simple, unaplogetically escapist and character driven. She likes to write loveable, redeemable and believable characters and place them in equally loveable, romantic and relatable settings and scenarios— removed from reality just enough so that the reader can properly escape, and even revisit!

You can connect with me on:

- https://www.cldonley.com
- https://www.twitter.com/C_L_Donley
- https://www.facebook.com/amarascalling
- https://www.bookbub.com/authors/c-l-donley

Subscribe to my newsletter:

- https://mailchi.mp/39ac5d9aaafb/love-on-a-lark-ml

Also by C. L. Donley

Leftovers With Benefits

My best reviewed book to date!

When Kenya's husband Cecil unexpectedly leaves her for a white woman, she finds solace with the most unlikely new ally: Kevin Hayes, the other woman's ex.

The Billionaire's Club Trilogy: Amara's Calling, Mya's Pride, & Kim's Courage

Amara and Grayson: the hot, quirky couple that started it all. Mya and Dale: the controversial pairing that no one saw coming, especially the two of them. Kim and Bel: the undercover royals who fall in love at first sight.

Spend all day in la la land jetsetting with this "plane Jane meets billionaire" trilogy about three couples that are as different as the individuals are from each other. Exotic locales, destination weddings, sex contracts, secret babies, and all the "happily ever afters" you could ever want!